Regina's Men

By Lynn Ray Lewis

ISBN-10# 1-945012-23-4
ISBN-13# 978-1-945012-23-5

Artwork by Jess Buffett Graphic Designs

Published by Vinvatar Publishing
Website: Vinvatar.com

Table of Contents

Prologue

Regina Simpson was a quiet young lady. She wore thick glasses, that hid her big green eyes, and had greasy, dark blonde hair. She had braces on her teeth, and a rather unremarkable, plump, fifteen-year-old body, that had yet to show any signs of womanhood.

Her binge drinking parents had finally made the headlines, but not in the way either of them had ever wanted. Witnesses said, that they were fighting when they left the party that they had attended that night. On their way home, her father had, somehow, lost control of the car. The vehicle had crashed through a guardrail, before it rolled multiple times, finally coming to a stop on its top. Both occupants were dead inside the car, when rescuers arrived.

The only relative that Gena had left in the world was a cousin who lived in Michigan. She was surprised when the cousin told Social Services that she wanted Gena to come live with her.

After three months in a foster home, the spectacle wearing, bookworm went to live with Olivia Fuller, otherwise known as Ollie, to her friends.

Ollie was twenty-two years old, and at first, the caseworkers hounded the duo as they got used to each other, and established ground rules. Within a few months the CPS workers stopped coming around, but left Ollie with a list of child counselors, just in case Gena ever needed to talk to someone about the accident.

They became almost like sisters, and when Ollie finally told Gena how she supported herself, Gena was shocked, but accepting. Ollie was a prostitute. Well, not really a prostitute. She provided men with certain experiences. Experiences that they had only ever dreamed about. Gena rationalized Ollie's actions as being an outlet for those dreams, so that made it okay.

Ollie explained to Gena that she had to stay in her room, with the door locked, while she entertained her clients.

"These men pay me a lot of money to make their fantasies come true, Gena. If they see you, they might not be comfortable. They'll wonder what's going on, and, as you can understand, most of them prefer privacy during our time together. Please understand."

Gena assured Ollie that it wouldn't be a problem, and so their lives moved on. Until the night Gena let her imagination get the better of her, and hid in Ollie's closet to see what all the noises coming from Ollie's room were about.

Gena watched the man Ollie called James, bend her over the chair, and heard Ollie beg the man to whip her ass. Watching her cousin enjoying herself, while a man used a short leather whip on her butt, intrigued the teenager.

James gave Ollie the whipping she asked for, before he twisted her nipples until the young woman screamed, and begged for more. He grinned as Ollie panted, and fell to her knees of her own accord.

She opened his jeans, and pulled out his cock, taking no time to do anything but stuff it in her mouth. When he felt her warm, wet mouth enclose the head of his penis, he told her that she was going to make him come.

He grabbed fistfuls of her light red hair, and pushed her head further down on his stiff cock. He said he loved the way she tried to take him deeper. And he moaned that he could feel the way her throat convulsed from her gag reflex. He pulled back enough for her to take a deep breath, and pushed his way back into her throat, thrusting deeper still.

"Take it. Take it all, you hot mouthed slut. You fell on my cock like the nasty slut I knew you were. I'm going to fuck your throat, and you're going to swallow every inch of me. You will suck my cock a little more to get every drop of my cum."

She tried to pull off, but his hands kept her in place until he was ready to allow her to breathe. He pulled back just enough for her to get air in her lungs, then buried himself as far as he could, and began pumping his sperm down her throat. Her throat worked his cock as it pulsed and choked her.

When James withdrew his flaccid cock from Ollie's mouth, Gena almost gave herself away.

The thing was still big as far as Gena could tell. She ignored the lure of sex in the room and the warm wetness between her thighs as she kept a hand over her mouth and continued watching to see what would happen next.

That was Gena's first introduction to sex education. There would be more to come over the next five years or so until Gena got through college, got a job, and an apartment of her own.

By that time, Ollie had graduated from college herself, and only took men with certain kinky needs on the side for extra money. She was twenty-seven years old, with a master's degree in business management, and she was still, technically, a virgin. Men had fucked her mouth and her anus, but none had persuaded her to give up her vaginal virginity. Ollie kept her clients on a strict regimen. They got what they originally contracted for and not a thing more.

As Ollie told Gena, "I plan to marry someone that I love, and although I might eventually be ashamed of my past behavior, at least I will be able to give the man I fall in love with that last little piece of me."

The men Ollie had been servicing weren't interested in regular sex. They had specific needs, and, as Ollie explained to the young Gena, she provided a service to those certain men. After all, most people with fetishes never got to play those little quirks out to see if they even actually liked it.

Ollie loved the feel of a man controlling her during the sex acts that she played with them. She needed a little pain at times, and was looking for a man who could enjoy the same kind of things she did. She loved to role play, and had several outfits for each role.

Chapter 1

Gena was feeling like shit. The company she worked for just downsized again and she was included in this wave of layoffs.

So here she was, once again telling Ollie her troubles.

"It's just like old times when I had a problem and I unloaded on you. It all seemed so much better after we talked. The only difference is, this isn't a bully or bitchy girl. I have enough money saved for the next three months, and then it's the soup line for me."

Ollie looked at her sweet cousin. She never regretted taking the girl in, helping her through those awkward teenage years, and then college. Gena had blossomed into a beautiful young woman, and Ollie was proud of her. Her stringy, dark blonde hair, was now beautiful, highlighted naturally with streaks of light blonde. Those awful thick glasses were no longer necessary after Lasik surgery, so her large, green eyes were clearly visible. The braces were long gone too, leaving a white toothed smile, with no overbite.

Her body had not gotten slender, but she had gotten taller. Her body had reapportioned itself into a generous hourglass figure. She was almost twenty-four years old, and was simply beautiful. Ollie loved her no matter what.

"Well, I have some news. It's better than yours, but I know you will be tickled to death about it anyway," Ollie said, grinning at her.

Gena finally left her pity party, and really looked at Ollie. The pretty redhead actually glowed with happiness, and Gena took a wild guess as to why.

"Who finally got you to fall in love with him? I can see it in your eyes. Oh boy, this is wonderful." Gena practically squealed the last few words when Ollie started nodding her head. "Tell me, tell me everything."

Over boxes of Chinese takeout, and two bottles of wine, the girls discussed Ollie's new man.

"He is six foot three, around two hundred and thirty pounds, and he has the most unbelievable muscles. I love to look into his brown eyes, and he accepts the no vaginal sex until we are married rule. I still can't believe it. After all these years of hoping, I finally found a guy that I can respect and love."

Ollie was lost in her thoughts again, causing Gena to laugh at her dear cousin.

"Oh, Ollie, I am so happy for you. So when are you getting married? More importantly, when do I get to meet him?"

"His name is Wesley Bradshaw," Ollie gushes. "He is thirty years old, and I love him so much it frightens me. I met him at that club downtown, you know the one I told you about? The one that makes you sign a confidentiality contract before they ever let you in the door?"

Gena couldn't believe her lovely cousin had finally found a man she loved, let alone found him in a private kink club. Ollie had offered to take Gena to the club sometime, but Gena was afraid that she might embarrass Ollie by staring at the women and men in various states of undress, that were doing some of the things she had witnessed Ollie doing in her bedroom with men over the years.

Ollie didn't wait for Gena to confirm or deny her knowledge of the club, she was still caught up thinking about her handsome husband-to-be.

"Wesley owns a company that manufactures some kind of patented doodad or thingamagiggy for cars. I actually have no idea what it is, all I know is that he makes a lot of money, and he can hold a conversation that doesn't include two references to a sex act in each sentence.

"As to how we met, well, I was hanging, ass in the air, getting a spanking, when he walked up to my date and was invited to join in. You know my rules, I contract with one man at a time, so the minute Wesley whacked my ass with his hand, my contract with Stuart was done. Stuart was so busy trying to impress Wesley that he forgot his obligation to me.

"As soon as the spanking was finished, he tried to fuck me. I threw out my safe word and everything stopped. Stuart had to let me up. I tried not to make a big deal about it, but he was stupid enough to challenge me there in front of Wesley and a few other people in the club. He followed me to the changing rooms. I was trying to get him to calm down. I repeated the terms of our contract, and then he called me a few names, including a prostitute, among others. I didn't raise my voice until he grabbed me and slapped me. The dumbass told me that I was just being used as bait anyway. Wesley Bradshaw is an important man, and Stuart went on to tell me his plan to get close him.

"He was so far gone, he never realized Wesley was outside the door with several of the men who know me. I don't know what they did with Stuart, I was too busy letting Wesley take care of my bruised cheek, and my arm where Stuart grabbed me.

"We have been seeing each other for three months now, and he proposed on Sunday. I swear, Gena, I love this man so much I can hardly believe he feels the same way about me. He knows about my little side activities, and said he could understand that I used them as an outlet for my own kink. The best part is that he is happy to give me what I need because he likes it too. So now we can both indulge in our fantasies."

Ollie was staring off into space again, and simply said, "He actually loves me, Gena. He loves me. He knows everything about me, and still loves me as much as I love him. I don't know how or why and I don't care. He makes me want kids and a minivan. I never thought that I would have that.

"I can even work for his company if I want. Wesley says he can always use a smart woman on staff to help build the company. He sees *me*, Gena. He actually sees me as a smart person, not just another pretty woman passing through his life. How could I not love a man like that?"

The wedding would be in Las Vegas a month from now. Wesley had to clear his calendar for the two week honeymoon. He was taking her to Europe to see the sights.

"I know how you can save some money. I own this condo, so you can stay here until you get a new job. After Wesley and I are married you can move in here," Ollie offered as she smiled at Gena like the benevolent fairy godmother she was to the younger woman.

Chapter 2

Gena saw the happy couple off at the airport and wished them well. She liked Wesley. It was reassuring to see the love and proud possession in his eyes every time he looked at Ollie. They made a handsome couple, and Gena could admit to herself that she was jealous.

Would she ever find a man that looked at her that way? A man that made her heart sing like Ollie said Wesley did for her?

As a parting gift, Wesley and Ollie had left Gena on a mini vacation there in Vegas for the next three days. The hotel was paid for, and she found a wad of cash in her purse when she had paid for her lunch at the hotel earlier.

Gena walked up and down the strip, amazed at the sheer number of people milling around and hanging out in front of businesses. She stopped at a small bookstore and bought two books, then went back to her hotel room.

One of the books she had purchased explained the different games offered in the Vegas casinos. She was fascinated with the author's insight about gambling. Never gamble when you are desperate, and know when to walk away.

After treating herself to four hours of luxury at the hotel spa, Gena felt like a million bucks. She had allowed them to talk her into having her eyebrows waxed, and she even got a Brazilian wax. That half hour was nothing but torture. She felt so exposed when the attendant ripped the wax covered hair from her body. They even waxed up the crease of her ass. She had to admit that her bare crotch was more sensitive and made her feel very sexy.

She slipped a heavily beaded dress over her head and zipped it up. She smoothed thigh high nylons over her calves and thighs, knowing she had never looked better, or felt sexier, than she did right now. The four inch stilettos made her ass and legs look fantastic, if she did say so herself. Grabbing a small clutch purse, and two hundred dollars, she went down to the hotel casino.

Gena stood back and watched the play at each table, trying to familiarize herself with the games she had read about in the book. When a space opened up at one of the craps tables she took the spot, and placed two, fifty dollar chips on two different numbers. When the dice came to her, she shook them lightly and tossed them down. Although she had no idea exactly what she had done, a pile of chips came to her, and she got the dice again. She added another fifty to the table, and the people surrounding her cheered when she won again.

Another pile of chips came to her and she decided to quit while she was ahead. She gathered her tray of chips and went to the cashier's cage.

Gena almost dropped her purse when she was given fifteen hundred dollars for the chips. Not a bad return on an investment of one hundred and fifty dollars. She didn't want to go back to her room, so she studied the slot machines next. The people that sat in front of those machines were an eclectic bunch.

She saw two, large slot machines side by side with no one playing them. They looked simple enough, so she looked around, opened her purse, and put a twenty in the slot that vacuumed the money out of her fingers. When she pushed the button the screen lit up, saying that the progressive jackpot was up to a million dollars. A maximum bet icon flashed on and off, but she ignored it and pushed the play button.

A siren sounded and clanging bells began ringing, while Gena looked around wondering where the noise was coming from. Two casino employees were coming her way, and she smiled at the men as they advanced toward her. She wasn't sure of their destination until they stood next to her. While she had been looking for the noise she had not paid attention to the machine that was actually making the noise. It was hers.

She stared, open mouthed, as her machine's display was showing gold coins spewing from a bank vault in animation.

After the noise died down, Gena realized she had to have won a sizable amount of money, otherwise, the two hunky looking men wouldn't have come over to her. She looked at the payout amount and her legs gave way.

"One hundred thousand dollars? I won a hundred thousand dollars?"

The men smiled at her and nodded. The taller man grinned widely.

"Yes, ma'am, you sure did," he confirmed, as he held her arm so she didn't fall.

When the strip of paper spit out of the machine, the shorter man pulled it out and gave it to her. He picked up her purse and handed that to her too.

The casino sent a photographer over while she was still stunned. She asked them not to publish the picture in any newspapers, and they reluctantly agreed. She did allow them to post the picture on the wall with other people's pictures who had also won sizable jackpots in the casino recently.

She made arrangements for the money to be deposited electronically into her bank account, and had them send the taxes to the IRS out of the winnings. She was left with roughly two thirds of the money. It was more than enough for her to live on until she found another job.

When she got back to her room she grabbed her cell phone to call Ollie. She knew her cousin's phone would probably be turned off, and was surprised to see that she had three messages from Ollie in her voicemail.

The three messages got progressively more hysterical.

"Call me."

"Dammit, Gena, Call me."

And the last message, "I am going to be in trouble if you don't call me as soon as you get this message. Call me."

Worried about Ollie and her new hubby, Gena called Ollie's number and waited anxiously for someone to answer. When Wesley answered the phone Gena hesitated, but curiosity won out.

"Hi, Wes, is Ollie available by any chance? I have some good news."

"Well, Gena, Ollie is tied up right now and can't come to the phone. So tell me what your news is, and I will tell you why Ollie was so frantic to contact you."

Gena was still concerned. Wesley sounded like he was upset, or mad, about something.

"Well, I just wanted to tell her that she won't have to worry about me so much now. I went down to the casino tonight and stuck some money in a machine. The next thing I know, I won a hundred thousand dollars. I am so excited."

Gena heard Wesley repeating her words and heard a muffled squeal in the background. The squeal was followed by a half a dozen smacking noises, and Gena could guess what Ollie was tied up in. She smiled knowing that Ollie liked nothing better than to be spanked. Just as she began to wonder if Wesley had forgotten she was on the phone he spoke to her.

"That's great, Gena. Ollie and I are both happy that you won't have to worry so much about finding a job for a little while. You do know I would give you a job at my company, don't you?"

She did know that, because Ollie had already told her that Wesley would hire her for something, even if he had to make up a new position. Gena knew the man had a big heart, and was once again happy that he had found Ollie.

"Yes, Wes, Ollie told me about your generous offer and I want you to know I appreciate it. So what's going on? Besides the honeymoon, I mean."

"You know about Ollie's hobby, right?" Wesley asked. "Well, it seems she forgot something until I mentioned that I have an important client flying in next week, and the following week we will be cutting the honeymoon short by a couple of days so I have a chance to meet with him.

"When I happened to mention his name, your cousin remembered that she had a contract with the man for three days this coming week, and had forgotten about it because they made arrangements for the meeting before she started dating me."

Gena could imagine that this must be a very awkward situation for Ollie, and especially for Wesley. His important client was expecting to get his fantasy, and the fantasy girl wasn't going to be there. When he met Wesley and

Ollie, oh boy, this could be a very bad thing. Now she knew why Ollie was in trouble with her husband.

She knew it was a bad idea, but Gena loved Ollie, and would do anything in the world for her. Even meet one of her clients to explain the situation.

"Since I am living at her place, why don't I take the man out to dinner? I can explain that his date with Ollie is not going to happen. He will understand, I'm sure. After all, what can he do about it now, especially since they probably haven't even met face to face yet, right?"

"Ollie should have cancelled the meeting with Trey as soon as she and I started to see each other. Instead she forgot about him, and now we're left with a mess."

Gena was hearing that Ollie had probably ruined her new husband's business with a thoughtless act. She thought of how happy Ollie was with the handsome Wesley.

"Wes? Look, I will just meet with him myself in her place. I'm sure he will understand when I explain what happened."

Wes refused to hear of Gena taking Ollie's place. She had no experience at all in the world of role playing, or BDSM. What if he seduced her regardless of her explanation?

"If that happens, it happens. I really doubt that the man who wanted a woman that looks like Ollie, would consider me as an adequate substitute anyway.

Chapter 3

When Gena returned from Vegas she stopped to get her clothes, before going straight to Ollie's condo. It took hours of phone calls and reassurances from Gena to Wesley, before he agreed to let her meet with Trey Fallon himself. Gena was as prepared as she could be. It was just dinner.

A few hours later she was sitting at the reserved table waiting for Trey to arrive. According to Ollie they were going to have a nice dinner together. When Gena had asked Ollie what brand of kink the man had wanted, Ollie hurriedly got off the phone without explaining.

Gena kept her eyes on the door, waiting for a tall, dark haired man to come in by himself. So far, she hadn't seen any man without a date or companion walk through the door.

She was so nervous that her fingers kept twining and fidgeting. When she realized she was beginning to panic, she put her arms on the table top and held her glass of water between them. The icy cold glass helped her redirect her emotions into something besides fear.

As she waited, she kept remembering some of her own fantasies. This was not exactly the place to get all hot and bothered, she had to keep her wits about her. Still, the anticipation of what it might be like to have a few of those yearnings come to life was exciting, and she blushed as she felt her nipples harden.

The thought that a man would want to spank her, or even use a paddle on her butt, excited her. Whether reality was as wonderful as her fantasies gave her to believe, was yet to be discovered. Ever since the first time she had spied on Ollie, Gena would slip back into her room and imagine that it was herself with the red butt cheeks.

She imagined it was she that a man had spread out on the bed or floor, licking and biting her pussy. Her favorite fantasy was born the night that Ollie almost gave up her long held virginity.

The man had been tall and good-looking. When he came in, they had a glass of wine before they retired into Ollie's bedroom. He'd ordered her to strip out of the tiny shorts and tank top she was wearing without a bra. He licked and bit at her neck and shoulders, pulling her by her nipples to the bed. Ollie had sat on the bed, and he continued to pull her nipples down until her face was even with his crotch.

His deep voice had ordered her to open his pants and take out his cock. He'd let go of her nipples and she had whimpered, but complied without hesitating to follow his orders. His hands held her head, while his fingers threaded through her hair as he directed Ollie to suck his cock. He'd praised her efforts, telling her what a good little cocksucker she was.

Gena didn't like that name, but he went on to call Ollie a horny little slut, and even a whore later while he was licking and biting at her wet slit.

Ollie was so lost in pleasure from his oral ministrations that she'd yelled at him to fuck her. Just before he began to slide his cock into her pussy, she pushed him back and said no.

The guy had grinned, and pulled her over his lap. He began to give her ass a hard spanking that had had Ollie in tears, and on the verge of orgasmic bliss again. He had spread her legs and finger-fucked her for a few minutes, using her own natural lubricants to drag up to her asshole, sinking a finger deep inside, while Ollie squirmed and squealed. She had let out a low scream when he added a second finger.

By the time Ollie was pushing her ass back onto his fingers, he was slapping her cheeks and thighs wherever he could reach without removing his fingers from pumping into her asshole. When he'd finally told her to get on her hands and knees on the bed, he began pushing his sizable cock slowly into Ollie's asshole, and Gena had felt the cream from her pussy soaking her panties as her own orgasm began.

Gena had had to bite her hand to stop from making noise, and alerting the people on the bed to the fact there was a spy in the closet.

After that night, Gena learned to enjoy the feelings that watching her cousin with her various men inspired. Often, she would go back to her own room and masturbate while reconstructing the scenes into her own fantasies.

*****

This idea had better work. Gena knew how much was riding on the hope that the man, Trey, accepted the switch of companions for the evening.

Tonight she wore a simple, but elegant, light pink sheath dress. It was made of a silky material that felt wonderful against her skin. She left her hair down, with only a slight wave to it, and her makeup was applied lightly to look as if it was barely there. Gena kept her fingernails long, tonight they were painted a light pink that matched her dress. Her toenails matched her fingernails, because she had been nervous and needed something to keep herself busy earlier today while she waited until it was time to get ready for this "date".

Gena didn't need to look at her watch to know that he was late. She resolved to wait another ten minutes, and if he didn't show, she would be justified in leaving the restaurant without further concern that it would anger him.

After the ten minutes were up, she finally motioned for the waiter to tell him that she would be leaving due to her date being delayed, when two men entered the restaurant. Both were tall and had dark brown hair. Both were simply drop jaw gorgeous, and after speaking to the hostess, both were headed her way.

The men stopped at her table.

"I'm Trey Fallon, and this is my partner, Quinn Edwards."

Gena felt the blush on her face, but there was nothing she could do about it.

"I am Gena, it's nice to meet you. Both of you."

The men each shook her hand and claimed a chair. The waiter hurried over and got their drink orders. Gena was surprised when Trey ordered a glass of white wine for her without even consulting her.

"Uh, excuse me, but could we change the wine to a whiskey and cola, please? I have allergies to some wines, and I don't want to end up at the hospital this evening."

The waiter looked to Trey for confirmation. Trey looked at her and nodded his head to the waiter.

"As the lady requests."

The waiter, damn his eyes, further humiliated her by asking for photo identification.

"I am sorry, miss, please understand that it is our policy, and I'm only a waiter here. I don't make the rules."

Gena was livid. She opened her purse, removed her driver's license, and handed it to the waiter.

"I trust that that is enough to satisfy your rules?" She knew she sounded sarcastic and that is exactly what she was aiming for. *This bullshit was going to stop right now.* When he dropped her cards onto the table in front of Quinn, Gena wanted to throw something. She had to half stand to reach the cards, picking them up to put back into her purse.

Giving the waiter a frosty glare, she told him, "Oh, and by the way, separate checks, please."

All three men tightened their jaws. If this wasn't so important to Ollie and Wesley, she would have gotten up and walked out of the place. How dare they act like she couldn't choose a simple drink for herself?

The waiter nodded and turned away to fill the order, as Gena glared at the two men sitting across from her. They, in turn, glared back at her until Quinn laughed.

"Buddy, I think we have a brat on our hands."

Gena had no idea what he was talking about. Brat? She was *no* brat. She was a twenty-four year old woman, and they had no right to belittle her.

When the drinks arrived Gena left hers sitting where the dumb fuck waiter set it. She ordered a steak, medium rare, with a baked potato and butter on the side. Let them order what they wanted, she was a woman in control of her own intake of food and beverage.

Trey broke the uncomfortable silence, "So you have allergies to wine? What other allergies do you have?"

It was an innocent question couched in a sarcastic tone of voice, and she smiled sweetly, giving him the list. Her allergies had been the bane of her life, and the source of her doctor's frustration.

"Well, I have an allergy to the acids that commercial wineries use to help break down the fruit during the fermenting process. It's not an allergy to the wine itself. I also am allergic to penicillin, most narcotic pain killers, latex, and long haired cats."

They weren't laughing now. Gena wondered why they looked at each other and back at her. This was going to be an interesting dinner date.

The waiter returned with their salad choices, and she ignored the men as she began to shovel the crisp greens into her mouth. Gena loved a good, green salad and closed her eyes, concentrating on the crunch and the burst of light flavors combining in her mouth. She licked the dressing from her lips, and opened her eyes.

Two sets of dark blue eyes were staring at her, and she blushed. Quinn had a forkful of his wilted spinach salad halfway to his mouth, and Trey had not started eating his salad at all.

She ducked her head, and ignored them until half of her salad was gone. Then she picked up her water and drank a few long swallows.

"So what do you guys do for a living?" That seemed like a safe enough subject and Trey picked it up.

"We manufacture quality, luxury vehicle, parts. We also dabble in other venues of manufacturing. Quinn and I own Alanark Corporation. Perhaps you have heard of us?"

She hated to tell them that she had never heard of them before, but why lie when all they had to do was ask a question or two and would know she was lying in the first place. No, it was better to tell them the truth, and see if the men had over-inflated egos to go with their control issues.

Gena shook her head, "No, sorry, I have never heard of your company, but there are a lot of companies I have never heard of."

They didn't seem to be offended by her statement, which was good, and the conversation began to get easier the more they talked.

They talked about several subjects, and when the subject of gambling came up Quinn got red faced when Trey ribbed him for losing at Black Jack in Atlantic City.

Gena had no intention of telling them about her big win in Vegas, but found the words tumbling from her mouth.

"I was in Vegas last week for my cousin's wedding, and after they left I was bored so I went to the casino. I learned to shoot craps, but I got so nervous I cashed my chips in. I found out that I won fifteen hundred dollars. Then I was wandering around, and I saw two slot machines sitting by themselves. I thought it would be a way to pass the time, so I put a twenty in the machine and pushed the button, bells and whistles went off, and I won one hundred thousand dollars.

"I just stood there like a deer in the headlights. I was looking around, trying to figure out where the noises were coming from, when two casino employees came over and helped me stand up, because my legs gave out when I finally realized that it was real."

She smiled in remembrance. "It couldn't have come at a better time you know. I had just been downsized where I was working, and I was worried about finding another job. Now, I can take my time finding something that I think I might like, instead of taking on just any job in desperation."

When dinner was over, Gena was so relaxed with the conversation, and with the attention of the two beautiful men, that the thought of them coming home with her, or her going with them hadn't even crossed her mind. At least it hadn't until they were waiting for the valet to bring the car around.

Trey held the door open for her to enter the car and she slid into the comfortable leather seat. Quinn slid in next to her, and Trey closed the door. He went around the car and got into the driver's seat. As they pulled into traffic, Gena folded her hands in her lap nervously.

Quinn sat back in the seat, resting his arm on the back of her shoulders, and without a word curled that arm around her, pulling her reluctant body to his.

"So, Gena, would you like to tell us why you met us instead of the experienced Olivia? Not that I'm complaining. You are certainly beautiful. And from the description we were given of Olivia, well, let's just say we are pleasantly surprised. Both Trey and I like a woman with hips and breasts.

"Are you ready to take on both me and Trey? Those lips of yours have been distracting me all evening. I keep picturing you on your knees, with my cock sliding through them."

He took her hand, flattening it open, and ran it down the front of his shirt over his chest. He pulled it down toward his belly, before she balled her fingers and tried to take her hand back. He held onto her wrist and continued on his way to his crotch.

Her knuckles brushed his fly, and she felt the hard bulge of his cock before she tried to pull her hand back.

He ran her fisted hand up and down the hard ridge watching her face and smiling.

"You never answered our question, precious. What is a sexy girl like you doing here in place of Olivia? And where is she?"

Chapter 4

Gena was shocked she hadn't offered an explanation sooner. It had to have been nerves, or the fact she was enjoying the undivided attention of the two men, as if they were actually there to meet her for dinner. She should have explained the situation up front just as she had planned.

"Oh, gosh, I am so sorry. I should have told you right off that Ollie was supposed to have called you to explain the situation. She was busy elsewhere, and I volunteered to have dinner with Trey so that she wouldn't feel so badly about standing him up. She never mentioned that there was going to be two of you. I think I would have remembered that small fact."

Gena decided to tell them a partial truth and hope it would be enough.

"Look, Ollie made the arrangements with Trey months ago. She got so caught up in a man she met, that she forgot all about your arrangements, and didn't remember until last week. When she remembered, she panicked, because she didn't want to stand you up, so I offered to meet with Trey and explain the situation. Ollie is on her honeymoon somewhere in Europe right now. That is why I volunteered to help out."

She hoped that she had answered the question to their satisfaction, because that was all they would get out of her concerning Ollie.

Quinn hadn't let her wrist go, and she tried again to pull her hand back, but he kept it shackled in his big hand.

"I think that it was really nice of you to volunteer to take your friend's place tonight. Are you prepared to take her place for the rest of the evening, too? Am I going to get my wish to see those beautiful lips of yours locked tight around my cock?"

She held up a hand.

"Just wait a minute, okay? I am not like Ollie."

*****

Trey kept his eyes on the road. He was having a hard time keeping a straight face. The girl was doing her best to protect her cousin and her new husband. He had to give her points for loyalty.

Six days ago Wes had called him. Wes told him that Olivia was now married and would not be meeting with him. From what Wes told him, her cousin was planning to meet with him for dinner to explain what had happened. They had some hair brained idea that he would hold it against Wes for marrying Olivia, thereby taking away his planned piece of ass for the three days that he had open between meetings.

As the men talked, Wes had told him about Regina, or Gena, as Wes called her.

"She is a girl with a body made for a man that likes curves, and she is completely clueless about her looks. According to my wife, her cousin is almost completely innocent, so don't make the mistake of expecting that she will be up for the kind of games you might expect a normal twenty-four year old to be experienced with."

Wes reassured him that he wouldn't be embarrassed to be seen with her at dinner. "The girl is beautiful."

When Trey had seen the woman sitting by herself in the restaurant, he had to agree with Wes's assessment of the girl's looks. She was indeed a beautiful young woman. Sage green eyes, framed with dark lashes, and eyebrows that were shaped in, what appeared to be, a natural wing design. Her mouth, with those plump lips did, indeed, evoke thoughts of hot sex. Her hair was a streaky fall of blondes, ranging from dark, almost brown, to ultra light streaks here and there. From what little he could see of her body he had liked it.

Trey liked a woman with large breasts. Many times he had enjoyed a woman with small breasts, but he preferred larger ones. Hers looked like they would be just about the right size.

Her little act of defiance at dinner had amused him more than anything else. She could barely look at him or Quinn, and yet there she was, sticking her chin up and declaring her independence.

Quinn was obviously fascinated with her. Right now, he was testing the waters, and Trey would bet the shy young woman would only increase his partner's appetite, not turn him off.

Trey had the address, and pulled into the designated parking space next to a small compact car that was dwarfed by his luxury model.

He got out of the car, as Quinn was pulling Gena from the back seat, helping her slide out. By the time Trey made it around the car, Gena was perched on the edge of the seat with her dress scrunched up almost to her crotch from being pulled over the leather.

The sight of white thighs and garters had Trey's interest centered on the hiked hem of that pink dress. Too bad she was already at the very edge of the seat. Another inch or so, and they would see if her panties matched the garters. She stood and gave her hips a little shimmy and the dress slid back down into place. *That was a shame.*

*****

Gena walked slowly to the door of the condo trying to pull her wrist from Quinn's hold without outright fighting him.

"I need my keys from my purse, if you don't mind. Let me go please." She was nervous enough about what might occur once they entered the condo, she certainly didn't need this man to act as if he owned her. It was just a date, or what she kept telling herself was a date.

She had been certain that once they knew she was a poor substitute for her beautiful, thin cousin, they would be in a hurry to leave her at the door. She still held out that hope, but something told her she was deluding herself. No wonder Ollie had gotten off the phone so quickly when Gena asked what nature of kink Trey Fallon liked.

A ménage had never crossed her mind. As far as she knew Ollie had never entertained two men at one time, but she had not always been at home when Ollie had guests.

Gena gave up attempting to liberate her wrist. She wouldn't give him the satisfaction of fighting him for something so simple. She comforted herself by calling him a control freak in her mind.

When they got to her door he released her, holding out his hand for the key she removed from her purse. Rolling her eyes, she handed it to him, and glanced at his partner, wondering if he was as controlling as Quinn appeared to be.

Trey was staring at her. His eyes seemed to be traveling from her feet to her breasts, where they rested for a few seconds, before traveling up to look into her narrowed eyes. He licked his lips and held out a hand indicating that she should precede him and Quinn into the condo.

Okay, Gena, you can do this. It's what you have dreamed about for years, and now it can be real if you just let it happen. After all, it's only three days. Think about how wet your pussy got all the times you watched Ollie with her men. Think about the way you envied her while those men ran their hands over her body, wishing it was you in her place. Think about the enjoyment you saw on the men's faces as they spanked her butt.

Gena told her inner devil to shut up. There was no way she could just have sex with these guys, even if they were the most handsome men that she had ever seen, and even if they inspired her pussy to weep.

Ollie had instilled, at least, some small measure of morality into her, and Gena remembered her mother telling her that one day she would find a man who would love her, and who she could love in return. She needed to remember that.

She stepped into the condo. She had to tell them goodbye, but that option was now moot, because Trey was right behind her, almost touching her, and they were both standing inside the threshold. She gasped and stepped back a few paces, which encouraged Trey to move further into the room with Quinn right behind him.

Gena stood waiting for whatever the two men planned to do to her. When they remained quiet, she looked up and grew more nervous as she saw them removing their suit jackets and hanging them on the backs of the dining room chairs.

Gena excused herself to freshen up and both men nodded their heads as if they were giving her permission to do so. She went into her bedroom to grab a clean pair of panties from the drawer, then she went into the shared bathroom between the bedrooms to change.

There was no way she could be comfortable with her panties being soaked like this. Gena quickly took care of her needs, including a wet washcloth to freshen up, before putting the new underwear on, and heading out to the living room where the two men were supposed to be.

*****

Quinn watched her walk toward the stairs and had to resist the urge to follow her. After Trey had gotten the call from Wesley, they had decided to keep their dinner plans, and then bum around the area for a few days. They had thought about dropping by one of the classier bars to pick up a woman or two to pass the time with. They didn't really have much of a plan until work and meetings took up their time.

One look at the blonde, with those shy green eyes, changed the game plan.

Neither man liked to play with the well used, and many times broken, submissive women that liked to hang out in clubs. The ones that were looking for the Dom of their dreams, someone to live up to their expectations. Not that those women were as disposable as they seemed to be. There were many men who looked for a trained sub, men who were too lazy to train one, or didn't have the time it took to train her.

Quinn and Trey knew exactly what they wanted. They wanted a woman that was submissive, with a streak of independence left in her. A woman that they could train to their hands, without her being so needy that she couldn't brush her teeth unless she begged for permission.

The knowledge that Gena was almost a total innocent at the age of twenty-four was a minor miracle. The fact she wasn't employed at this time was another plus for them. If they played their cards right, and she liked the experience of having two dominant men controlling her pleasure, she might consent to leave with them when they went back home.

Quinn recalled Wes telling Trey of the scheme the women had hatched up together in an effort not to piss off Trey. He and Trey had laughed about it at the time, but now that little plan might work to their advantage.

In reality, Trey would never pull his business from Wes's company as long as they continued to produce high quality parts. In fact, this trip was to see if the company was equipped to retool without major renovation to accommodate another part for Alanark Corporation. It was ludicrous to think that the loss of a strange piece of ass, contracted for only three days, would cause Trey to ruin another man's business.

Many times when Trey or Quinn were going to be away for a few days, they would call the local private BDSM club in the area, if there was one, and ask for a sub that wanted to play for whatever length of time they would be in the area. That was how Trey got connected with Olivia. Her particular kink of ass and mouth penetration only was a weird one, but the men could deal with that. It was no hardship to fuck a well trained mouth or asshole. As long as she lived up to her reputation, she would have been perfectly acceptable as a companion for the weekend.

It had been dumb luck that Olivia forgot about the contract and married Wesley.

*****

Gena walked into the living room feeling scared and excited, all at once. First, she would try to reason with them, if that failed, she would at least be able to tell herself that she'd tried. The way they looked at her made her blush, and she could feel her labia tingle, as her nipples hardened.

She offered to make coffee, but neither man wanted any, so she sat on the arm of an overstuffed chair and started to talk.

"I'm glad that I substituted for Ollie tonight at dinner. The food was delicious. I'm really sorry she forgot to cancel your plans for this week. When she met Wes, uh, her husband, every thought in her head seemed to have gone by the wayside. I told her that you would understand once you knew the reason for her absence."

Chapter 5

Gena thought she had her story straight, yet she had almost screwed it up by using Wesley's name. The men didn't seem to notice the slip and she was keeping her fingers crossed that they would leave soon. Her nerves were already shot from a full day of worry and anticipation. Now all she had to do was get them to leave and life could get back to normal.

"Gosh look at the time, it's almost nine o'clock. I bet you guys are tired and probably need to get settled into your hotel rooms."

Trey shook his head and said one word, "Strip."

When she stared at him in surprise he repeated himself, adding, "If you don't, I will be unhappy, and Quinn will be devastated. We are not going to do anything to you that you don't want. So do as I tell you, girl, or I can strip you myself. You might be a substitute, but I believe that we got the better deal by getting you instead of your cousin."

Gena stood and reached for the hem of her dress. The material soothed her as she fingered it, trying to decide whether she should, or even could, comply with his order. Her natural inclination was to do as he said. This could be a no strings affair, and she would finally know and feel all that she had been missing. Or, she could take the smart way out and tell them to leave.

She didn't believe they would hold her decision against Wesley. These men looked too confident to let a little thing like the loss of a woman that they had never met cause them to take their disappointment out on a man that loved his wife.

She felt Quinn step up beside her, taking one of her hands in his. She looked away from Trey's face and swiveled her head toward Quinn.

His lips landed on hers just as she opened her mouth to ask him what he thought he was doing. His tongue explored her mouth, as his hands cupped the cheeks of her ass and squeezed. His tongue kept sliding over the ridges of her teeth and the roof of her mouth, he licked at her tongue, engaging it in a duel of touch and retreat. By the time he allowed her to surface for air, the pale pink dress was unzipped and hanging from her shoulders. He moved in for another breath stealing kiss, and Gena vaguely felt a soft breeze over her shoulders as the dress was pushed off completely, falling down her body to land on the floor at her feet

Quinn's lips left hers and traveled to her neck, nuzzling and licking as he went. When her bra loosened she squeaked and he made shushing noises to try to soothe her.

"Remember? Nothing you don't want. Do you want me to stop? Or do you like it when I do this?" He asked as he cupped her breasts in his big hands, lifting them slightly to kiss and lick each nipple in turn.

She gasped and moaned, pushing her chest toward that pleasure giving mouth of his. *Oh, goodness.* No wonder Ollie loved having a man lick her body. The sensations had her pussy leaking its cream into her panties again, but she wasn't going to stop him. She wanted this. For once in her life she was going to do what she wanted and worry about consequences later. All those years of watching but not participating. Wanting, but being afraid of not being good enough, or skinny enough, for a man to truly want her, would be put to the test tonight.

This wasn't prom night, and neither of these men resembled the fumbling boy who thought if he came she should have too. He was a selfish prick, with no scruples, and fewer brain cells.

Quinn kept touching her body, running his hands up and down her arms and back, while his mouth kept her nipples at attention.

His lips left her breasts, making her whimper, as he kissed her neck and shoulder.

"Let's turn you around so Trey can see what he's been missing, baby. He is sitting there with a hard-on from just seeing your sweet ass in those pretty little panties. Show him how wet the thought of having the two of us touching you all over, and eating that hot pink pussy between your legs, makes you."

His hands turned her, as he ran his fingers down her belly to her hips.

"You see the way his nostrils are flaring? He likes eating pussy more than just about anything. We will let him unwrap that creamy cunt of yours, while I play with these beautiful breasts. You'd like that now, wouldn't you, Gena? Tell me this is what you want, baby."

"Why don't we find your bed and get comfortable."

Quinn picked her up and carried her up the stairs, turning into the room that she had gone into earlier. He was certain it was her bedroom, and he was right. The queen sized mattress was kind of small for what they would be doing, but it didn't matter in the long run. They could lay her out on the carpet if they needed extra room.

Chapter 6

Gena woke up to the sound of a man snoring. She was startled to find herself sandwiched between two masculine bodies, radiating heat and keeping her sides warm. She smiled as she recalled the activities of last night.

She wondered why the men hadn't fucked her last night. They had been as intimate as three naked people could be, and yet, even though bodily fluids had been exchanged, neither of the men's pricks had penetrated her.

Her resolve to experience sex with two real men last night hadn't been fulfilled. She remembered the feelings of ecstasy that these two men had evoked in her and she felt her cheeks warm. When Trey's mouth had licked her pussy, while Quinn had distracted her with his thick cock, she had been full of confidence in her ability to please the men. They seemed to know her body better than she did. Her nipples were still sensitive, and she felt the whisker burns on her inner thighs. She remembered the fingers in her butt hole, and felt shame at the pleasure that she had felt. Her jaw was a little sore from trying to take Quinn's thick prick into her mouth. It was a bloody miracle that she didn't have a sore throat to prove that her throat wasn't built for the beautiful blunt head of a man's cock.

Gena levered herself on an elbow to toss one leg over Trey's torso, feeling with her toes for the floor. Her leg was stretched as far as she could get it before her toes made contact. She crab crawled from between the men without disturbing them.

She grabbed a thin, silky robe from behind the bedroom door, and slipped into the small hallway. She made her way to the kitchen to start a pot of coffee. While it brewed, she went to the guest bath and took a much needed shower.

As she lathered her hair and rinsed it, she thought about what might happen next. The men knew she wasn't really substituting in the contract with Ollie. There was really no contract now.

As she dried her body with a fluffy pink towel, she wondered again why they hadn't fucked her. She looked in the mirror and saw several small bruises on her neck, and what appeared to be fingerprints, dotting the flesh of her breasts.

She looked down at her thighs, spreading her legs to see if she was marked there. It didn't matter how she contorted her body she couldn't see a thing. Not that it mattered. She could still feel the whisker burn to remind her of the pleasure of a man's mouth on her.

She brushed her teeth, combed the tangles from her wet hair, put the robe back on, and went back to the kitchen.

As she sipped her coffee, Gena wondered how long the men would sleep. She wandered into the living room and noticed that her dress was lying on the carpet in a heap along with her bra and shoes. She felt her face flush as she remembered the way Quinn had peeled her dress off last night.

She had had no idea just how wonderful it would feel to have a strong man holding her, taking control, causing her body to want anything he was willing to give her.

Admittedly, her body was already priming itself for sex before they ever walked into the condo. After the attention from the two handsome men at dinner, and the way Quinn forced the issue with her hand touching him intimately, even if it was through the material of his slacks, the scared feelings mingled with the excited feelings.

To be totally honest with herself, from the first moment that she had seen the men she knew she would do whatever it took to have at least one of them show her what all the fuss was about. There was nothing rational about her decision. They could have been rapists, and she wouldn't have known it until the last minute. She had allowed lust and need to overcome logic, and was fortunate that the men hadn't harmed her.

It was the dumbest thing she had ever done in her life, but it was also the most fulfilling. She also knew that given the chance, she would repeat the same mistake with the two men. No matter how she tried to talk herself into backing out, Gena had wanted the experience with the two of them. It was why she hadn't put up an argument when they decided to have sex with her. Unfortunately, they'd had sex, but not really.

She picked up her scattered clothing and took it to the laundry room. The dress would have to be dry cleaned, so it went into the laundry bag to be dropped off.

She went back to the kitchen to pick up her coffee mug and refill it. Just as she reached for the coffee pot, she felt a large warm body at her back, with thick muscular arms wrapping around her waist and ribs. The whiskered cheek nuzzling her neck made her giggle.

"Good morning, pretty lady," Quinn said before he moved his hands upward to cup her breasts, while his lips traveled between her shoulder and ear.

His fingers pinched and rolled her nipples, slowly applying pressure, until she had to breathe through the pain. The feeling seemed to shoot from her breasts straight to her pussy, and she felt the moisture leaking into the gusset of her panties.

She groaned and leaned back on his chest, giving him an open invitation to nibble on the rest of her neck if he wished. Instead, he lifted her up and deposited her onto the breakfast bar lengthwise, pulling the robe from her arms and leaving it under her so that the cold granite countertop would be covered. He arranged her hands over her head, padding her wrists with a kitchen towel, and tying the towel with the butcher's twine that he had found on the counter by the stove. He used the pan hooks under the island to tie the ends of the twine so her arms would stay over her head.

He grabbed the seat of the barstool nearest to him and placed it at the end of the countertop. He raised her ankles to the counter, but that did not suit him until he pushed her thighs apart, holding them wide.

"Now this is a beautiful breakfast. All warm, and with just a little stirring, the cream will be ready for me to lap up. I know we are told not to play with our food, but, baby, I plan to play as long as I want this morning."

Quinn sat on the stool, and proceeded to give her slit a long, slow lick.

"Hmm, you taste so good." When his fingers pulled the thick lips of her labia back he began a narration of what he was doing.

"I see a beautiful pink pussy that is making my mouth water." His fingers squeezed the flesh between them and released the pinch, repeating it over and over, as his tongue slid from her clit to her anus. His fingers abandoned their play with the puffy lips, as one finger slid inside the moist heat of her silky cunt, while its counterpart played with her clit.

Gena squealed, trying to raise her hips. The feeling of being spread open on the kitchen counter like this was so exciting.

"Oh, please, what you're doing feels so good, don't stop. Please don't stop. Yes, what you're doing with your mouth." Gena knew she was babbling but she had no words to describe the feelings that she was experiencing. His tongue began to penetrate her and proceeded to stab inside while his finger continued to torment her clit.

Something brushed her hair making goosebumps appear on her skin and when she looked up, Trey was watching his friend eat her out.

Gena watched Trey's hands rise to cup her breasts. They overflowed his hands, but he held the undersides in his palms, while his thumbs and the first two fingers on each hand grabbed her nipples, pinching and rolling them. He began pulling them up and applying more pressure to the tender buds until she screamed, feeling the beginnings of her orgasm tightening her muscles.

Her hips pumped as much as Quinn's shoulders would allow. Two of his fingers slid inside of her entrance, pulling it wider as her muscles contracted around his fingers, and his mouth worked its magic on her clit.

Trey kept pressure on her nipples even as she fell over the ledge into the best orgasm she had ever experienced. When he finally let go of her nipples, the pain from the blood rushing back into the nubs bowed her back, as she rode out the aftershocks on Quinn's fingers.

Trey bent down and took her lips in a tender kiss.

"Did you like that baby?" His hands rubbed her breasts. "Did you like the way Quinn ate your beautiful pussy? I liked watching your pleasure take you over. I remember how good your juicy pussy tasted last night, and watching him enjoy your cream just makes me want more. Look down at Quinn. Go ahead, look."

Gena raised her head and looked at Quinn with his head lying on her mound and thigh. He was staring at her with heat in his eyes, as he licked his wet lips. She whimpered. He looked so handsome, in a ferocious predatory way, that she didn't know what to say. What could she say to let them know how much she enjoyed and appreciated the pleasure that they gave her.

Trey untied her wrists and helped her down from the counter.

"Why don't you go and change into some clothes and we will take you out for brunch?"

She opened her mouth to ask if they wanted her to try to please them, but his words stopped the offer before she spoke. Nodding her head, she left the room and went upstairs.

Opening her drawers and picking out underwear made Gena laugh at herself for wondering if the men would like them or not. She chose a shell pink bra and thong set, knowing that the color looked good against her pale skin. She put cream on the newest set of whisker burns on her inner thighs, as she thought about this morning's activities.

Trey and Quinn certainly knew how to bring her body more pleasure than she ever dreamed of. She had thought Ollie had experienced the best orgasms, but there was no way her cousin could have ever felt the depth of pleasure that these men gifted her with.

Still, there was a nagging feeling that something was holding them back from the ultimate pleasure of fucking her. It was obvious to her that they were capable of using their cocks. Neither man had any reason to worry in that department. Only a couple of the men she had seen with Ollie were as well endowed, or even close to as large, as these guys were. Thinking of their beautiful pricks gave her goosebumps. Both last night, and again this morning, the evidence of their arousal made it clear that they weren't unaffected by giving her pleasure, or in the case of last night, allowing her to return the pleasure.

They had been expecting the beautiful, slender Ollie. That must be the problem. There was no way she could compete with her cousin if that was the reason.

Gena stood up and walked over to the full length mirror on the inside of her open closet door. As she looked at her reflection she knew that her assumption must be correct. Her thighs were much thicker than Ollie's, and her breasts would never fit in a man's hands without spilling over his fingers. Her waist was thicker, too. She was all curves and well padded flesh, where Ollie was a sleek size two.

Well that was too bad. She refused to be jealous about it. She might admit to herself that there was a certain amount of envy for the lost opportunity of experiencing the promised pleasure of a man's cock inside of her body. Yet she couldn't feel remorse for enjoying the pleasures she had already experienced. Maybe someday she would find someone who loved curvier women. She had read about them, but had never encountered one, that she knew of. At least none that had been attracted enough to approach her as of yet.

Telling herself to stop wishing for something that wasn't going to happen, she made up her mind to treat them like visiting friends. They had been to the city before, so they probably knew that weekday entertainment was a bit scarce until after six at night.

Today was Friday so the bars and clubs would be open and filled with college students. Or there was the Opera and Symphony, but most of the time you needed to get tickets weeks, if not months, in advance, unless you wanted to sit in the balcony and watch little figures walk across the stage.

She would have another meal with them, thank them for a lovely time, and get on with her life. She dressed in black Capri slacks, with a pale peach t-shirt that had a sweetheart neckline. A hint of cleavage showed, but since

she was covered decently she didn't worry about it. Sliding her feet into rope thong sandals, she made her way downstairs and stopped dead in her tracks on the bottom step.

The men had changed into jeans and t-shirts themselves, and what a sight they made. Wow, men with muscles, sexy hair, and sexy bodies encased in clothing that showed off how yummy they looked. Before she could stop herself she let out a long, shrill wolf whistle in appreciation.

"I swear that I will have to fight off the women. You two should be labeled as menaces wherever you go. Should I bring a stick to beat the girls off the two of you?"

Gena stepped down off the stair, and advanced toward them, before moving two feet to the right, and heading for the door. She grabbed her keys from the small side table, and pocketed her ID and credit cards, before heading out the door.

She was giggling as she made her way to her little compact car. The looks on their faces was worth the small amount of teasing. Teasing men was fun. Not that she was in the habit of doing so, but this idea of treating them like friends calmed her nerves. This was familiar footing. She had male friends, most of which asked her questions about other women. "Do you think she likes me? Should I wear the blue or the red shirt?" Shit like that she'd dealt with since junior high school. She was always the girl that would listen to their problems.

Always ready to offer up advice on subjects she had no business pretending she knew anything about.

This was different, but men were men no matter their age. Praise them, especially the ones that don't actually know how attractive they are, and they will be your buddy for life. No pretense, and no expectations from them. Damnit.

The hand on her arm, spinning her around, wasn't totally unexpected. The sharp smack on her ass made her squeal in laughter.

Trey pulled her back to his vehicle.

"You can ride with us. We wouldn't want you to get lost on the way home. Our suitcases are inside your condo."

Chapter 7

They stopped at a large chain restaurant and ate brunch. Gena was surprised at the amount of food the men ate. She just had a normal sized omelet and coffee. They ordered, what appeared to be, half of the breakfast menu, scarfing down every slice of bacon and every bite of potato that was set in front of them.

Over a last round of coffee, Trey told Quinn that he knew how to get to Greenfield Village so they wouldn't need a map. "I called ahead and scheduled us for a tour at two o'clock this afternoon. We can get a good idea if the new parts will be feasible to put into trucks too. That way, when we make our pitch to the automakers, we'll know what we're talking about."

The men discussed the applications for some of the new innovations that their engineering department had come up with, and Gena had to wonder what she was doing there. As she sat and listened to them discussing the possible placement of the new parts, her eyes wandered over the patrons in the restaurant.

No one was paying attention to their table. The two waitresses were standing behind the counter rolling silverware into napkins. Two older men were talking in a booth. And several businessmen were scattered throughout the room.

She excused herself to use the ladies room and left the table. After washing her hands and finger combing her hair, she returned to the dining area and watched her men stand when she approached them. She felt quite proud of herself for not melting into a puddle at the sight of the two sexy men that smiled at her when she rejoined them.

They left the restaurant, and drove to Dearborn. Before she knew it, she had shared the story of how she came to live with Ollie.

"It was funny when she came to my school functions. My male teachers forgot I existed and focused all of their attention on Ollie. All the football players would stand around with their chests puffed up trying to get her to smile at them so they could brag to their friends. Billy Sutton actually bet that he could get a date with Ollie when I was in my senior year of high school.

"She was so nice to him that he didn't mind being rejected. She patted him on the cheek and thanked him with a kiss on the other cheek, before telling him that she had a boyfriend. His friends acted like he had actually scored with her the way they carried on over that kiss on the cheek."

The men shared that they lived in Madison, Wisconsin. They had a company that developed luxury parts, such as onboard bar fixtures and vases, that could be permanently affixed to the interior of a vehicle. They designed high end, personalized metal gates for luxury homes, and a host of other items for the wealthy. They also had made two fortunes in the stock market.

"Just before the economy went bust, we decided to invest in apartment buildings. Before the paperwork had been drawn up for a particular building with one hundred units, the property was foreclosed on.

"We waited a few weeks, before we stepped in. We paid pennies on the dollar for the same property. We updated the units, and raised the rent. We eliminated two of the apartments, and added a gym for the renters. In the next building that we purchased, we knocked out two more apartments and put in a small diner that starts serving breakfast at five. They're open for lunch, but at night they are busy delivering pizzas, burgers, chicken, and whatever else they can think of to cater to the people in the apartments."

Gena found the Ford River Rouge plant to be fascinating. The manufacturing process was enlightening. Between the huge robots, and the friendly people explaining the process, she had a great time. She was happy to see people working, too. She knew what the economy had done to most manufacturers, she was just lucky enough to have her job last longer than many others had. The economic fall, had taken four years to catch up to her ex-employer.

After the tour, on the way back to her place, Trey parked outside of a small, square brick building, situated between a strip mall and a car dealership. She wondered why they stopped, but since they seemed to know where they were, she didn't voice her curiosity. Quinn went inside the building while Trey sat in the car with her.

She hated the silence, so she began to ask him questions.

"So, what do you like to do for fun?" She knew the minute the question left her mouth that it had been the wrong thing to ask. She blushed as he looked at her and slowly grinned. "I meant other things; you can't have sex every free minute of your life. If you did, you would be worn out by the time you were twenty-five, and since neither you, nor Quinn, look any worse for wear, I assume you go to the gym or participate in sports." She stopped looking at his grinning face and stared out of the window.

*****

Trey knew it was a bad idea, but he got out of the driver's seat and opened the back door, sliding in next to Gena. He stayed near the door, pulling her shoulders around to face him, then he pounced. He took possession of her pouting mouth, in a complete mouth fuck. He groaned as her little tongue joined his. When he sucked her tongue into his mouth, refusing to let it go, she was moaned. His hands held her breasts, as his thumb and forefingers tormented her nipples. He let her tongue go with a sigh, before his head drew back.

He pulled her by the nipples down toward the seat. He let her nubs go, while he arranged the top half of her over his lap, with one of her legs bent at the knee on the seat, and the other one planted on the floorboard.

"When we get back to your place, Quinn and I are going to teach you a few things about what we like to do in our spare time. For example, I love the taste and textures of a woman's body. I love to lick, pinch, and suck a woman's breasts. I find your breasts to be addictive," she whimpered as one of his hands left her breast to cup her pussy. "I loved the taste of this prime pussy that I ate last night. I plan on licking up every drop of cream that I can coax from it today, too. You will spread yourself for my mouth. Your cream is delicious. So much so, that I will probably still be eating you, while Quinn is stretching your asshole so it can take his cock easier than if he just shoved it inside of your sphincter. I have seen that happen, and trust me, you will be glad he doesn't want your first anal experience to be all about pain and embarrassment. We want to give you as much pleasure as you can possibly take, and then make you take even more.

"Do you feel the connection from your nipples to your cunt? I can feel the way your pussy is creaming through your pants." His fingers unzipped and unbuttoned her Capris, so his entire hand could slide between the waistband of her clothing and skin.

"There is the little button that will give me all of the cream I want." His thumb honed in on her clit giving it a wiggle, while his fingers continued to her slit. His thumb stayed to play, tormenting her clit while his fingers began playing in the moisture that they encountered.

The feelings his fingers were coaxing from her body made her squirm and writhe on the seat. She tried to arch up, to force his fingers to fill her vaginal opening, but he set the pace. She wanted him to finish his game and let her experience that same stars-bursting-behind-her-eyelids feeling. She wanted him to give it to her without delay.

"Please, I need to come. You make me feel so needy."

His thumb pushed down on her clit, keeping pressure on it, as his fingers drove just inside her small, slick opening. The orgasm crashed through her until her belly cramped from attempting to take his fingers deeper, the walls of her pussy clasping onto his fingers.

Quinn opened the car door as she sobbed through the release that those wonderful fingers had given to her.

"Oh fuck, man. Keep her warm and ready until we get back to the condo. Seeing her enjoy your hand playing with her slit, has my cock ready to blow. I have everything we need, plus a few extras just for fun."

*****

Gena felt embarrassed by the way the men talked. When Trey urged her to turn over until her face rested on his knee, she was certain he would want her to suck his cock. She reached her hand toward his zipper, intending to let it loose from behind the confining cloth, but he pulled her hand away, shaking his head at her.

"Not yet, little one. You need to learn to ask for what you want. I have told you that we like a compliant sub, not one that grabs for what she wants. You just earned yourself a spanking when we get you home."

She felt his big hand slide under the waistband of her pants, squeezing one of her ass cheeks, then the other. A long finger followed the slit between her cheeks, and down through the wet lips of her pussy, that were too lubricated with her body's juices to offer any resistance. By the time Quinn parked the sedan in the parking lot of the condo, she was raising her hips in counterpoint to his fingers pushing inside of her body. She felt like crying when his fingers left her wet depths. Her protesting groan was met with a sharp slap on the ass. That got her attention and pissed her off. She sat up and scowled at Trey as he opened the car door and climbed out, extending a hand toward her to help her out of the vehicle. She ignored his hand, instead giving him a dirty look as she scooted out of the opposite door to stand across from the two men.

"I am a human being, and I don't like either of you right now. This has been a mistake. I want you to get your stuff and we can forget this entire thing." She turned her back on them and marched to the condo.

Once she fished the key from the small pocket at the waistband of her pants, she finally got the door open. The men were scowling as they walked inside the condo, but didn't say a thing. She wanted them to argue with her. She really wanted them to beg her to change her mind. They sat down on the couch and glared at her instead of gathering their things.

What did they expect now?

When Trey crooked his finger at her she scowled back at him, before walking into the living area, standing with her arms crossed at her chest, waiting for someone to speak first. When they continued to stare at her she broke. This wasn't what she envisioned her first ménage experience to be. Bossy men who made her body feel like she could barely walk, tormenting her until she wanted to scream at them to fuck her, and stop torturing her like Trey had done.

She liked the feelings that the men evoked in her, but the torture, making her wait to orgasm, that was just mean. While the idea of a spanking made her pussy leak even more wetness, the bossy way the threat was made had her resenting the good feelings she was beginning to enjoy.

"I've enjoyed the things you guys have shared with me, I'm not going to lie, but even though the thought of being spanked is exciting, I resent being treated like my wants don't count. I wanted to make you feel as good as you made me feel, and I got threatened with a spanking for trying to pleasure you. I get teased until I feel like I will fall apart if you don't finish what you started, and I get a smack on the ass instead of the pleasure I expected. I don't want to play these lopsided games. If you can touch me anytime you want and tease me into a blubbering mess, I should have the right to tease you, too." There, she had said her peace, if they couldn't live with her demands they needed to leave.

She would just masturbate in the shower, as usual, and regret this weekend for the rest of her life. She stepped back when Quinn stood, advancing toward her. The slight smile on his lips bothered her. Her heart thudded as he pulled her into his arms, and without hesitation put his mouth over hers, clamping his teeth over her bottom lip, pulling on it, until she opened her mouth to say something. His tongue swept into the suddenly dry cavern as she gasped for air.

Within minutes, or seconds, she was no longer keeping track of time, she felt her clothing being removed, and moaned. She needed to, at least, pretend she objected to the way they seemed to be ignoring her feelings. She clamped her teeth down over his tongue, just enough to get his attention, and got her nipples pinched for her trouble. He held the tender tips, rolling them between his fingers as his lips left hers to travel to the soft skin beneath her ear.

"So, you want to pleasure us like we pleasured you? Get on your knees. Show me how you plan to pleasure me. I'm going to sit in the chair, and you are going to suck my cock. Make sure you're careful, for every time I feel your teeth, you get five smacks on the ass, added to the ten you've already earned from Trey."

He stripped the clothing from his body, and Gena got a good look at the complete man. The thought that she may have taken on more than she could handle filtered through her mind when she saw his thick cock standing at attention in front of her face.

Giving herself a little pep talk helped, but she was very careful when she wrapped her hand around the base of his cock and licked the wide head. He pulled her hair up and out of the way so he could watch her mouth close over his flesh, and she got a thrill when he moaned. She remembered the way Ollie played with men's cocks, and began to tickle his shaft with her tongue, especially around the little bunch of skin just under the head. He jerked and sighed when she did it, so she did it again, but this time she added suction just to feel his reaction.

"Oh yeah, babe, you can suck like that, it feels great. Back off a minute while Trey gets ready to play. I bet he's going to finger you good, in both your holes, that way we can both sink our cocks inside of you later. I picked up plenty of lube, and non-latex condoms. I also got a few other items we might find helpful."

She felt fingers smearing something cold and wet down the slit of her ass, and onto her clit. Trey pulled her knees up one at a time, putting them on the sofa cushions that he had taken from the couch. It raised her ass up higher than her head, that was currently resting on Quinn's thigh. Her legs were placed so wide apart that she could feel the cool air wafting over her inner pussy lips. It was an odd feeling, and she tried to close her legs. That idea was nixed quickly with a sharp slap on her ass, and a growled warning to stay where she was.

She licked at the long prick resting next to her head, trying to distract herself from the feeling of the long, thick fingers penetrating first her pussy, and then her asshole.

The first wasn't too bad since she had been treated to a few thorough climaxes last night that involved her body clasping around fingers and tongues. The finger pushing its way into her ass was uncomfortable. He continued to finger fuck her rear hole and as she began to get used to it, he added a second finger.

She gasped a, "No, it's too much," at first, yet when he began to widen her tight ring, she felt the cream flow from her vagina. She began

65

to push her hips back and forth as he pushed his fingers deeper, twisting them until she squealed. She wanted more. She pushed her ass onto his fingers, her body demanding more, even as she began sucking on the skin of Quinn's shaft. The hand holding his thickness began to shuttle up and down as she licked and sucked, moving her hips at the same time.

When Trey pulled his fingers out of her sphincter, she whimpered. She heard plastic being torn apart, the sound sharp to her ears, but refused to give up the flesh in her grasp to bother to look. Quinn tasted salty and a little bit like soap, but she wanted to feel him come apart under her labors. She had the power here, they weren't going to reach satisfaction until she was damn good and ready.

When she felt something cold and smooth at her empty asshole, she sighed, and began to pant. Trey was pushing a dildo into her ass, and she tried to breathe through the burn and slight pain. She held on to the knowledge that this was just like when his fingers had widened her. There would be a slow burn, but then this toy would give her pleasure as soon as she was used to the size of it. It wasn't really that much larger than his fingers, and she got used to the thing fast. When he added his other hand to play in her soaked vaginal tunnel, she couldn't stop the orgasm from washing over her body.

Chapter 8

Quinn took his cock away from her hand and mouth after having her learn what he liked her mouth to do. She was strangling him and he planned to fuck her first. Although she was certainly doing a good job of giving him oral sex, he wanted her to learn to suck his head inside of her mouth too. She needed to learn many things and he was in the mood to teach her, just as Trey was. His partner kept grinning each time he introduced her body with something new. He must be getting the reactions he'd hoped for. It didn't surprise him when Trey stood and headed to the bedroom with the bag of tricks he purchased earlier today. He had to grin to himself when he thought of the enjoyment they would have in the coming hours. Reaching for her hand, he stood and drew her to her feet before sweeping her up in his arms and walking to her bedroom.

Trey insisted on allowing her to have a moment to think before they proceeded. He was the one that had to work everything out in his head, and on paper. His brain worked in numbers. Pluses and minuses, pros and cons, he needed everything to add up. It wasn't a bad thing when it came to business, but it was damned inconvenient when it came to times like this. Quinn was ready to see how far they could take the little virgin.

"Before we continue with this, I want to hear from you that you consent to what will happen. You need to know that we are not a couple of raw boys here. At times, I thrive on seeing a woman roped and tied for her men's pleasure. We enjoy bringing a submissive woman to her knees of her own freewill. If you say yes, you will discover a great deal about yourself. We will help you achieve more pleasure than you ever believed possible, just by trusting us, and letting go of your control.

"Now is the time to say something, before we start. You either accept what we are offering, or it stops now." Trey sat on the bed, waiting for her answer.

He knew she was feeling pretty desperate right now, but he needed to hear her say it. They needed to know that she could be brave enough to acknowledge her needs to them, and to herself.

She had been too lost in the pleasure to have be aware of her sweet pussy dripping her liquid over his fingers as he had played with that beautiful asshole of hers. Even the initial press of his fingers into her tightest hole had had her creaming all over his fingers within seconds. The little virgin thrived sexually when she had a small dose of pain with her pleasure, and that suited his sadistic side just fine.

He could hardly wait to clamp her nipples. Trey wished that Quinn had bought a crop at Dolly's toy store. Striping her ass, as she rode Quinn's thick cock, would amp up all of their pleasure. She was in for a treat, all she had to do was say yes, and he was ready.

Pulling the bag to him, he began to pull a length of silky rope, and a red scarf, from the plastic sack. He grinned when he found simple, silver nipple clamps in the bag. He set those on the bed next to him. Her eyes were glued to his hands, itemizing everything he pulled from the white plastic bag. The large box of condoms had her eyes widening, but her mouth dropped open when she saw the two butt plugs still in their packaging. The two packages of batteries actually had him looking questioningly at Quinn.

It seemed he had some powerful ambitions for the evening's entertainment. Where he had a touch of sadism in his needs, Quinn liked to dominate. He could convince their chosen submissive that ignoring his directives was almost a sin.

"Gena, we're waiting. No one is taking your decisions away from you. If you want what we have to offer, say yes, or say no if you aren't interested. Either way, it's time to decide. Do I go into the bathroom and take care of the hard-on you caused? Or should I wait until we have you hot enough, and completely ready to take both of us?" Quinn sat next to Trey on the side of her bed.

She was torn, the opportunity to experience everything she wanted to try was sitting right in front of her. Her hesitation was not because she didn't want what they were offering, it was because she wanted it all too much.

"Alright, yes. I want to enjoy sex with the two of you. My big hang-up here is the bossy way you keep acting. You seem to think I am going to just fall on my knees and kiss your asses when you click your fingers. No one has ever had that kind of power over me, and no matter how many times I try to tell myself it will be alright, I feel like I will lose a part of me. My self-respect and independence mean a lot to me. Ollie is the only one I have ever been able to rely on before." She hung her head and whispered, "I'm scared."

Quinn couldn't believe she hadn't talked with her experienced cousin about the power exchanges that took place during a Dom/sub relationship. Trey looked like he was about to pounce on her, ready to show her instead of telling her what she needed to hear. He was all about choices most of the time, but she had admitted that she wanted them. Now Quinn wanted to make sure she understood what she was getting herself into.

"Do you see this hard-on? You are the cause of it. Look at Trey, his cock is in the same shape as mine, and you caused that too. You have the power here, you can make our bodies go as haywire as we can yours.

"I get a sexual high from dominating a submissive woman, I won't lie. Trey here gets his enjoyment from seeing a woman enjoying a bit of a bite with her orgasms. When we

70

stopped off earlier, I made sure to get the condoms that are latex free, because you said you were allergic. If not for your allergy, we would have had this discussion last night, and would have already begun enjoying each other. You have no idea how it makes a Dom feel when his sub places her trust in him, and in his judgment to guide her pleasure.

"Not to mention, the pleasure it gives a sadistic Dom like Trey. He will give you pleasure, mixed with just enough pain, to make you orgasm like you never have before. Your pleasure is our pleasure. And ours is yours. That is the simplest way I can put it without breaking out the videos and picture books."

That certainly explained why they hadn't had intercourse with her last night. She liked that they had listened, and remembered her allergy, it gave her a warm feeling. So far they had given, and given even more pleasure, yet she had only scraped the surface of theirs. The time to do this, or not, was here.

She chose to drop to her knees, placing her hands on her thighs palm up, as she had seen Ollie do so many times. She refused to look down though, if this was an exchange of power, she was equal to them and planned to stay that way.

When she sat back on her heels, she was reminded of the plug in her butt, and she winced. The pressure was a strange feeling, but she liked it. Her pussy was weeping in happiness and excitement. She looked at the two men and smiled, nodding her head in agreement.

Quinn let a small smile grace his lips, before he crooked his finger at her and she went to all fours. Somehow, from someone, she must have had a little training. He would ask her about it, but not right now. There was so much to do with what time they had together now. She was moving slowly, with a grace he had not seen before, as she crawled toward the bed. Her breasts swayed with the movement of her body, and he remembered the clamps Trey had already taken from their package.

Trey pulled her upright by her arm, and she found herself draped over his lap, belly down, legs spread, with her face in Quinn's crotch. The feeling of him pulling the butt plug from her asshole made her anticipation level skyrocket. She began to lick the inside of Quinn's thigh, remembering that she wasn't allowed to touch his prick without permission. The first smack across the cheek of her ass stung, the following smacks were fast, bringing tears to her eyes, as more liquid slid through the lips of her spread pussy, leaking onto Trey's leg. When he slapped between her legs, it sounded like he had slapped a puddle of water. It stung a bit, but excited her too. He pulled her cheeks further apart, adding more lube to her rear entrance, before he pushed a larger plug slowly inside.

Quinn used his cock to tap her cheek, and she took it into her mouth. The salty taste didn't bother her, she was actually happy to get her mind off the bigger plug stretching her asshole. The gurgling noises she made seemed to delight the men. She took as much of the cock in her mouth as she could, before reaching to wrap her hand around the shaft, but she was promptly rewarded with a smack on her ass for the effort. So she propped her torso up on her elbows, and tried to suck Quinn's thick prick deeper, raising and lowering her head. She was able to take him to the back of her throat, and even a little beyond before she gagged. She saw this as a personal challenge. Ollie had taken men's cocks until her nose met their pubic hair.

If Ollie could do it, so could she.

Her ass was on fire. The plug was being slid slowly in and out of her, while she sucked on the cock in her mouth. When Trey pushed the thing in all of the way, she screamed.

Holy fuck that hurt.

Before she could yell at Trey, Quinn had his hand on her head pressing her over his cock, cutting off her scream, and filling her throat, as his prick was shoved further into her throat. Her clit was tapped, and fingers filled her wet pussy, as she felt the pulse of Quinn's cum squirt down her throat.

Before she could take more than a deep breath, after Quinn's softening prick slipped from her lips, she felt something warm and rounded at her vaginal lips. It kissed just her lips twice, before penetrating slowly inside. The feeling of the condom was odd, almost as if Trey was stuffing her with a very large dildo, except this was no dildo. Even with her being as slippery as she was, the condom-sheathed prick had to work to gain each inch. Back and forth, side to side, he was driving her insane with need, and the fullness that only a hard cock could cause. She felt him push inside, gaining depth, continuing until she had taken his length as deep as he could go. She gasped, trying to adjust to his thickness, but he began pulling out and pushing back in, too fast for her to catch her breath.

He kept gliding over one particular spot, that felt like an electric shock every time he rubbed over it. When Quinn pulled her nipples, she broke. She began her own rhythm, throwing Trey's off, as she shoved back onto Trey's long cock. Sweaty tears ran down her cheeks by the time her arms collapsed over Quinn's thighs, as Trey was making short jerky jabs at her cervix. She laid there, savoring the feeling of his cock pulsing in rhythm to the semen shooting into the condom as he came. Those small jabs were uncomfortable, but felt wonderful at the same time.

Trey was still deep inside of her when she felt the first slap of his hand on her ass cheek. By the time he had spanked her ten slaps, she was backing her butt up into the smacks. She whimpered, latching onto Quinn's cock, and sucking strongly.

He groaned, but let her have her way. He lifted his hips, forcing her to take him deeper, and in turn, lighten her suction on the head of his cock. He felt the back of her throat and pushed a little more. She started to gag, but didn't back off, as she kept trying to push her head further down over his pulsing prick. With a loud moan, his cum sluiced over her tongue. He felt her swallow, the motion putting pressure on the head of his cock, stimulating it even more. He twitched as she kept sucking even after he'd emptied his load into her greedy mouth. He grabbed a handful of her hair and pulled upwards to make her let go of his prick.

Seeing the triumphant gleam in her eyes, he knew they had exactly what two men like them needed. She might have been virgin tight, but she was as into them as they were her. Her ass kept rising, and he could see that Trey was enjoying the ride.

Trey cursed as the condom began to pull off on the out-stroke. He pulled away only long enough to yank it off, wipe down with the sheet, and then replace it with a new one. While she continued to circle her hips and moan, he repositioned his cock and slid smoothly inside, enjoying her little growl of pleasure, as she backed into the stroke.

Quinn reached behind himself, and grabbed the nipple clamps. Her eyes were closed, but when he let go of her hair and palmed her breasts, she made a strangled sound and whimpered. He found her nipples, and began pulling and twisting them lightly. When he clamped the first nipple she groaned, while the second clamp had her screaming, shoving her ass back at Trey, and demanding that he go harder and faster.

"Fuck me. That hurts, oh God, fuck me harder."

Quinn saw that she was ready to come as her movements became jerky, and her mouth hung open in a low screaming groan. He grinned to himself, while he pulled the clamps from her, enjoying the show as she went wild, hunching and swearing through the pain of Trey's long cock kissing her cervix, as well as, the blood rushing back to her nipples.

Monday morning came too soon for Gena. She knew this weekend had been a gift. She had thrived under the direction of the men, not to mention the punishments.

Remembering last night's episode had her tightening her thighs together. She had been tied wrist to ankle. Spread wide open while Quinn licked her begging pussy. When he'd gotten her to verbally beg to be fucked, he had removed the plug from her anus, and stretched her hole with his fingers. He had teased her while Trey watched and made suggestions.

When he had finally begun to enter her sphincter, she had wondered if having a cock in her ass was a good idea after all. Ollie had sworn that it was better than anything she had ever felt before, but that was way before she had met Wesley.

Quinn had worked his prick into her tight hole, as she huffed and tried to breathe through the initial pain of his entrance. The butt plug had been smaller than Quinn's prick.

"This hurts, it hurts bad, your cock is, oh God, I want more. No, wait. It burns. Deeper, if you stop I-," she had screamed as he pushed the last few inches inside of her burning hole.

Once he was seated as deep as it was possible for him to go, she'd readjusted her ass to make it more comfortable for herself. She could feel her own body grabbing at his flesh, and she began to squeeze his fat cock inside her ass. There was still pain, but the fully stretched sensation made it worth it.. She'd tried to pull back a little bit, receiving a smack on her ass for her efforts.

"Stay still. You'll get your turn to fuck my cock in whatever hole you want soon enough. Right now, I'm in charge of this tight asshole of yours. It belongs to me." He started with slow, short strokes that teased her sensitive nerves. When he had worked up to deep, strong pumps of his hips, she'd begged him to fuck her harder. He'd stopped in mid stroke, using his fingers to spread the lips of her pussy.

"Hey, Trey, want to help our girl out here? Look at the way her pussy is trying to find something to fill it."

She could feel the way her vaginal tunnel was clasping on nothing, weeping from the lack of something to hold onto. When Trey slid two thick fingers inside, and pressed his thumb down over her clit, she came unglued. No amount of discipline could have stopped her from planting her feet and raising her hips, while she screamed out her pleasure.

She was going to miss the men who had introduced her to herself. She might have enjoyed being submissive to them, but she knew who held the power these past few days. Had she ever thought that the men would worship her body like they had, she might not have wasted time in dropping to her knees that first night they'd arrived. Her introduction to their talented cocks was icing on the cake. They would become a wonderful memory that she knew would stay with her for years.

She'd gotten out of bed an hour ago, took a quick shower to wash off the semen and saliva from her skin, then she had gone into the kitchen to brew coffee, and make a quick coffeecake for their breakfast. They would be leaving the condo today, and the knowledge made her want to cry.

They were great guys, at least they had been to her, even if they were a couple of bossy Neanderthals. They had a midmorning meeting scheduled with some people, before they were meeting with Wesley in the late afternoon. Then, they had a late night flight back home tonight.

This morning was the last she would see of them. The coffeecake was her own recipe and it turned out perfectly. She set out cups, small plates, and the cake on the kitchen table, while she checked her emotional state. Can you fall in love, with two different men, in under three days?. It didn't make any sense to feel like this, but when they walked out the door, she would grieve.

Arms surrounded her from behind, and she knew it was Trey who held her by the scent of his cologne. The man smelled like the first fresh breeze of a warm Spring day. She turned her head to kiss his jaw, as he lowered his head to rest it on her shoulder. His hands were holding her breasts, and her nipples were being tormented, as he seemed to love to do.

She drew in a shaky breath, "I made coffee, and coffeecake, so you guys would be wide awake for your meeting this morning."

He let go of her breasts and turned her to face him. After a deep kiss, he let her go with a sharp smack on the ass. They talked about the weather and the fact Ollie would be returning today.

Yesterday, they'd gotten her to tell them the truth about her cousin's marriage, as well as, the plan they had initially come up with. After an ass cheek burning spanking, they had made her apologize on her knees. As far as punishments went, it wasn't much incentive for her to regret her actions. Her pussy had been sopping wet before either man shot his load over her breasts, and down her throat. The minute she had confessed that she was on the birth control shots, they'd fucked her at the same time. The feeling was unbelievable. There was no way she could have ever imagined the fullness and raw pleasure, of the orgasms that resulted from the double penetration of the two thick pricks. They had held her afterwards as she cried from the beauty of the experience. They had thought that they had hurt her, but she assured them that it was the opposite feeling. After they washed her, the men took turns cuddling her close for the rest of the night.

Quinn came into the kitchen and she poured him a cup of the fragrant brew setting it on the table before he grabbed her close for a nicely satisfying open mouthed kiss. The men ate large slices of the pastry and drained the pot of coffee, before carrying their bags to the door.

"If you guys come back this way, be sure to call so we can have dinner or something. It can be my treat." She wanted them to leave so she could get her crying jag over. She could feel it building deep in the back of her throat. Her eyes were burning with unshed tears.

After another round of nipple pinching, and ass squeezing, they left her standing in the doorway waving goodbye to them as they drove from the parking lot. The tears were falling before they even reached their rental car.

It was a good thing that the condo was the last on the block of buildings, and the neighbors were gone for the winter. She cried and beat on her pillow for, at least, an hour. She tried to convince herself that it had just been lust. Nothing more. However, the memory of their eyes and smiles, tormented her for hours.

They were used to new, sexually submissive partners, wherever they traveled. She told herself that it was no big deal. "You got the education that you wanted, Gena. You wanted it, you begged for it, live with your decision." Lying to herself would do no good.

81

Logic told her to suck it up and move on, that there were men all over the place. If she wanted companionship, she could find one somewhere.

She spent the day in the condo, cleaning and changing the bedding. The last thing she wanted was to have their scents on her pillows and blankets, while she tried to sleep. The phone rang again, and this time she picked it up. Nothing but dead air, just like several other calls she had answered in the last week. It was slightly unsettling, but considering that the phone was in Ollie's unpublished account, she figured it was one of those robot callers, and forgot about it. The phone continued to ring most of the day, so she turned off the ringer. If any calls came in for her, they would be on her cell. Not on the house phone.

When Ollie called her late in the afternoon, they talked about the honeymoon and Wesley's skill as a lover. Obviously, her cousin was still high on married life and ready to settle into domestic bliss with her ultra masculine husband. She wanted to share her weekend exploits with Trey and Quinn, but for some reason she couldn't make herself interrupt Ollie's gushing stories from her perfect honeymoon.

How would she describe her time with the two men? As the perfect fuck date, or as an educational, hands on seminar? She decided to say nothing unless Ollie asked.

Instead, she discussed the possibility of investing her winnings in a business of some type. "I'm thinking of, maybe, looking into buying a restaurant, or a bar and grill. I'm not sure exactly which, but I love to cook, and people love to eat and drink, right?

"I have a business degree, I should be using it. The money I won in Vegas will help me when I go to the bank for a loan." It was actually an old dream of hers to own a place like she was talking about.

She wanted a place where people gathered and laughed. Hopefully, in a neighborhood where repeat customers would come in and she would already know what they planned to order. A place with a postage stamp sized dance floor, and a dartboard in the corner. Maybe there would be room for a pool table.

She loved the idea of taking care of people, even if she only listened to their problems. As a child she had been fascinated with the shows on television where the bartender would assist the cops, giving them information, or the ones where everyone greeted a regular customer when he walked in the door. Those places were always friendly, and no one called people names or shunned each other. If a person came into her place it would be for company, and to meet friends. With the right area, the right demographic, and the right menu, she could make it happen.

She was still lost in her plans when Ollie giggled and told her that she needed to have dinner ready when Wesley got home, or be ready for a spanking. They made plans for a girl's day out before hanging up the phone.

Sleep wasn't easy to come by for the next week. She dragged ass around the condo only going out for a few groceries, and to check her mail. Ollie was supposed to meet her on Sunday so that they could go through Ollie's old room and sort out what she wanted to take with her. Everything else she planned to donate or throw away.

"After all," she told Gena, "I can't see myself donating used vibrators and riding crops, can you? If I donate my costumes to the women's shelter they will have a cow," she joked.

Saturday morning she showered, before deciding to go to the store to stock up on junk food and wine coolers for Sunday. She picked up the mail, and stopped by the bank to get some cash. Most of the time she used her debit card, but sometimes she needed cash for the pizza delivery guy. By the time she got back to the condo, she was shaking her head wondering what had possessed her to buy so much food. There were four bags of assorted grocery items, and a stack of scandal rags to keep her updated on who the latest Hollywood sluts were. One even had an article about the growing popularity of BDSM ménage relationships.

It had started to rain, so she tossed the mail into one of the bags, that way she wouldn't forget it and have to make another trip to the car, and ran for the door. By the time she unlocked the door and got everything inside, she was soaked. She tossed the frozen items into the freezer before heading into her room to peel out of her wet clothes. She didn't plan on going anywhere else today, so she put on a soft, fleece lounge pant set. She shoved her feet into the gorilla slippers, that Ollie had given her last Valentine's Day, to warm up her feet.

The late Spring rain was too cold to enjoy, or laugh at. May was normally the month when Michigan began to come out of hibernation, but this year had been especially cold. Mother Nature was bitch slapping them this year for sure.

She finished putting away the groceries, gathered the mail and scandal rags, along with a steaming mug of chamomile tea, and headed for the living room just as the doorbell rang. She set everything back down and went to the door.

No one knew she was here, except Ollie and the two men that she couldn't get out of her head. The men that had left an assortment of sex toys in her dresser drawer. Toys that she couldn't resist using in the wee hours of each night, when her body craved what they had easily given her.

She looked through the security peephole, seeing a man in a brown uniform and cap. What on earth?

She opened the door and immediately tried to slam it shut. The man had a gun pointed at her midsection and strong-armed the door to keep her from shutting it, even with all of her weight behind it. Luckily, she was desperate enough to give the flat wood one final shove with all that she had, and the door went almost to the jam. The wrist holding the gun was pinned between the wood of the door jam and the door itself. She was not about to give any ground, and kept pushing the door with her body until the gun dropped onto the floor. The man's screaming at her to let go of his hand became too much for her to listen to. She leaned forward a tiny bit, and slammed her body against the door until she heard the bones in his wrist break.

He wouldn't be able to grab a gun, or anything else with that hand, for the time being, so she eased off the door, letting it fall open just enough for the hand to disappear, before she shut and locked it.

She ran to get her phone and call the police. While she was still talking to the dispatcher, she pulled the largest butcher's knife from the wooden block on the kitchen counter, and sat where she could see both the balcony door, and the front door. If he somehow managed to come back and try again, she would be ready for him. She left the gun where it had dropped.

She had always intended to take a gun safety course, but never remembered to look up the information she needed for the classes. That was going to change. On Monday she would be making the necessary calls. She felt so stupid, and when the police got there, she was surprised to see one of them held a box that had been outside of her door. He asked her if it was addressed to her, and after looking at the label, she nodded her head. When she looked at the return address, it was an unknown address from Wisconsin. The only people she knew from Wisconsin were Trey and Quinn. How had the pretend deliveryman gotten the box? More importantly, why did he want to attack her of all people?

Chapter 10

She could hear more sirens in the parking lot, and the officer told her that they had found the real deliveryman around the corner of the condo. He was alive, but barely. Someone had beaten him with an unknown object and left him, probably believing the man was dead.

She answered all of their questions, and gave them the contact information for Ollie. They praised her for her quick thinking, they told her that they wished more women could handle themselves as well as she had. But she didn't feel like a tough woman, she was shaking inside, and sick with worry that the guy would be back.

"He will be back, I heard his threats, and when I finally gave that last big push, I heard the bones in his wrist break. He was cursing, and yelling at me that he would be back. I'm surprised that the people down the block didn't hear him scream."

The cop laughed and spoke into the radio on his shoulder. The officer dusting her door heard what she'd said and chuckled.

The first cop crouched down so that she wouldn't have to keep looking up to talk to him. He wiped the tears running down her cheeks and looked into her eyes, "You did good. You saved yourself, and hurt him bad enough that he will need to see a doctor or go to a hospital.

Do you understand what that means? We will be able to find him simply by contacting the medical clinics and hospitals in the area. If that doesn't flush him out in the next few hours, then hopefully the statewide bulletin will. He won't get far if you heard the bones break like that. I'm going to let you in on a little secret too," she tilted her head and he must have known that he had her attention.

"This guy has been on the loose too long, he has beaten and raped four other young women in the past year. You are the first big break we have to find him now. He won't have the opportunity to get to you again. You'll have police protection around the clock until we get him. Tomorrow, an officer will pick you up, and if we have him in custody, we will ask you to pick him out of a line up. If we don't have him, our artist can get a drawing of him to help find him. Does that sound like something you feel like doing?"

She nodded her head and thanked him. It was past dinnertime by the time they left. There was a police cruiser in the parking lot, with a policeman watching the condo for any suspicious activity. It was almost anticlimactic to be left on her own again. She looked at the forgotten box on the table, and pulled it to her.

It was a small box, not much bigger than a shoebox, and she wondered what was inside. She took the box, along with her collection of mail and magazines, to the table in the living room.

The room was already darkened, because one of the policemen had drawn the drapes over the sliding doors that led outside. He had also made certain that that the broom handle was solidly in place to block the door from sliding open, even if it was unlocked. She turned on the overhead lights in the room, before going back to make another cup of tea. She also made a turkey sandwich to go with it. Not that she was hungry, but it was something she needed to do. The last thing she needed to happen today would be for her blood sugar to drop.

As she ate the sandwich and sipped her tea, she opened her mail. There wasn't much there to worry about. The electric bill was in Ollie's name, but she would pay for it herself. Cable, credit card, and an envelope with her name scrolled across the top line. *Hmm, interesting.*

She smiled when she realized it was from Quinn. It was a simple thank you card, with a message saying that he missed her, and wished she was there to keep him warm because it was still cold where he was at.

She set the card aside, but kept glancing at it, smiling as she pried the tape from the box. Seeing the cloth padding, that kept the smaller boxes from moving around, had her gaping at the beautifully worked nightgown. The embroidery on the hemline had to have been hand stitched. No machine could have done such a beautiful job of mixing the jeweled colors. The nightgown was snow white satin, with erotic depictions of women on their knees in various submissive poses. It made her wish they were there to see her wear this elegant garment.

The smallest box held a pretty set of three earrings, she knew they weren't intended as such, but the gold knots on each end of the posts made her shiver a bit. These would be for her nipples and clit. The thought went straight to her vagina, and she could feel the dampness leaking into the pants she was wearing.

There was a beautiful choker in another box, and one more box contained a bicep cuff. The etching on the cuff mirrored the depictions on the nightgown. She'd left the largest box for last. It was almost the full length of the box it came in.

Opening the lid, she almost dropped the contents. The metal shone brightly, but the etched pictures, again, showed women in lewd poses. Portions of the metal cylinder were raised in the shape of a man's penis, and once she saw the flange at the base of the thing, she realized it was a butt plug. It was not as big as either man, but it was so close that the idea of wearing it deep inside of her small hole made her juices flow even harder.

In the same box, there was a set of silver balls in the shape of cherries. They were pretty baubles, and she held them in her hand, staring at them. It took her a couple of minutes, but she finally figured out what they were for. As with the butt plug, she set them back into the box, then she put the rest away too.

Handling the items made her wish the men were with her to teach her how to use them. If they kept sending her things like this, how would she ever forget them? She took the box, and the beautiful card, into her bedroom and put them in the dresser drawer next to the other sex toys.

As she finished her tea, someone began knocking on her door and ringing the doorbell. It took several moments, and a few deep breaths, for her to gather the courage to check the security peephole. She saw Wesley and Ollie and yanked the door open as quickly as possible. Ollie rushed her, hugging her tightly, while crying and blubbering about coming home with them, so they could keep her safe.

She embraced her overly emotional cousin, and looked around for Wesley. He was prowling around the sliding doors, testing them to make sure they were locked and secure. He went to the windows in the small dining area, then he disappeared up the steps, presumably to check the bedroom windows as well.

She pulled back from Ollie, and was immediately drawn back into her clinging embrace. She tried to make soothing sounds and rubbed the smaller woman's back to calm her.

"I'm fine, he didn't get a chance to hurt me, and he has a broken wrist now. There is a cop sitting outside to take him to jail if he is dumb enough to come back. I'm fine, really."

Wesley came back into the room, shaking his head with a small quirk of his lips. She gave him a narrow eyed look, as he came over to them, pulling Ollie away from her.

"Look, honey, Gena is fine, and she had everything under control. Why don't we all go into the living room and sit down so you can tell her our good news? You want her to know about that, don't you?"

It was amazing to see her cousin cry like her heart was breaking, but smiling at the same time. Wes led her over to the deep padded armchair, and pulled her onto his lap, running his hand up and down her back.

Gena went into the kitchen to get some cokes for her and Ollie, and a beer for Wesley. By the time she came back, Ollie was resting her head on Wesley's wide shoulder, almost asleep. This was just too weird even for Ollie to do. The woman was Attention Deficit Disorder poster worthy most of the time. She could make a humming bird look lazy. Something must be wrong to make her so docile. Well, something more than what had happened here tonight.

Wesley accepted the cold drinks, popping the top of the can for his wife, before twisting the cap off his beer. He shook his head, and came out with it.

"What Ollie was planning to tell you tomorrow, is that she's pregnant. She took three of those over-the-counter, pee-on-the-stick tests, and it showed positive for pregnancy on each and every one of them." He grinned at her and winked. "She has been an emotional wreck for two days, and I thought it was strange to see the busy bee sleeping during the day, so I started asking questions. I bought three different versions of the at-home test. I insisted she try to use them this morning, and she has been crying ever since. She says she's happy, but can't stop crying. I managed to get an OBGYN appointment for Wednesday. If she was doing this on purpose, I would give her something to cry about, but she can't seem to help it, so she's getting a pass.

"Now, tell us what happened," he demanded. "I got the phone call, and Ollie insisted we come over here, to make sure you were in one piece."

Gena was stunned. Ollie was the most loving, beautiful person in the world. She was so happy when she finally found Wesley. Now they had a baby coming, too? Gena jumped up, and drummed her feet on the floor turning in a circle, laughing and pumping her fists in the air.

"This is great. I'm so excited." She ran over to Ollie, pulled her off Wesley's lap, and hugged her tightly. The crap events of the day were all but forgotten, as she gushed about how wonderful it was that they would have a tiny person around.

Wesley watched the way Gena finally got his wife to stop crying. If he'd known that Gena could work that miracle so easily, he would have brought Ollie over as soon as they had seen the results.

After the meeting with Trey and Quinn, he'd wondered what had happened over the weekend. Both men looked relaxed and rested, but he had been too rushed to make small talk with the men. He still needed to return a call he'd gotten this morning, but the drama of finding out he would be a father in around eight months, put everything else out of his mind. Since the call from the police came in, this was actually the first relaxing moment he had enjoyed the entire day.

Ollie looked ready to drop by the time Gena offered to fix them something to eat. They declined, and Wesley took his wife up to her old bedroom so she could take a nap. He laid down with her, holding her until she slept. He hadn't expected to fall asleep too.

When he woke up and remembered where they were, he left Ollie sleeping while he went to the bathroom. Then he went down to the kitchen to ask Gena why she hadn't woke them. The clock by the sink showed that it was just after one in the morning. Gena was sitting at the dining table drawing something.

He grabbed a beer from the fridge, and walked over to where Gena was. She was concentrating so hard that she jumped when he pulled a chair out and sat down. It was his turn to be surprised when he saw the sketch she had been working on. He knew this guy. He was the fucker that had escorted Ollie to the club, and lost his membership that same night for ignoring a sub's safe word, and becoming violent when she told him no.

What was that bastard's name? Shit, once he'd set his eyes on Ollie, everything had stopped for him. There was no mistake, it was the same man. Gena had captured the close set eyes, and Slavic cheekbones perfectly. Even with the ball cap, there was no doubt.

"Is this a picture of the guy that tried to attack you today?"

She nodded her head, biting her bottom lip while she studied the picture she'd created.

"You need to call the police and tell them that we know who he is. I recognize him from the club. I can't remember his name, but Ollie might. As soon as she wakes up, we can ask her. He's a weasel. I can picture him abusing someone smaller than him."

"The officer told me he has been doing this for a few months. He said there have been four other women that weren't as lucky as I was. His threats had me frightened, but Sergeant Mitchell assured me they would be able to catch him. He'll need medical attention to set his wrist. I was so scared, but I kept shoving my ass against the door to keep him from opening it. When I saw the gun drop, and heard the bones crack, I let his hand go. With a

name, the police should have an easier time of finding him.

"I planned on making panini's for dinner, but if you'd rather have something else, I can feed you frozen pizza, or an omelet."

He sat with her, while they discussed Ollie and his work. He casually mentioned that he needed to call Trey, and she turned pink at the mention of the man's name. Uh oh, it seemed he'd hit a sensitive spot there. Her head went down, and she studied her fingernails, but never offered a word pertaining to the dinner, or anything about the weekend. He changed the subject, slightly relieved when she excused herself to go lay down for a few hours. She thanked him for staying, and surprised him by giving him a quick hug, before disappearing up the steps, into her bedroom.

She couldn't sleep. The contents of the drawer were calling her name, but with Ollie and Wesley in the condo, she wasn't about to masturbate. Gena didn't want to risk making too much noise. With the day's happenings, and as emotional as Ollie was, they might come busting into her room, to discover her using the vibrator, or even the newest toy, that had been teasing the back of her mind since she'd opened the box and discovered what was inside.

She must have dozed off, because it was light outside when she opened her eyes, and she could smell coffee brewing. Looking at her

bedside clock, she saw it was already eight o'clock, and she had company.

By the time she made it downstairs, the handsome Sergeant Mitchell was sitting at the table with Wesley, drinking coffee and chatting about the sketch she'd done in the early morning hours. The men smiled at her as she poured a cup of coffee for herself, and walked over to join them. When she glanced toward the living room, Ollie was lounging sideways in the big overstuffed chair, reading the scandal rags she had purchased the day before.

"Good morning. I take it Wesley called you with the good news? I see you have the sketch I drew last night. Did you catch him yet?" She hadn't meant to shovel all of her questions at the handsome officer like that.

He assured her that they were still looking for the man that Ollie had identified as Stuart York. Wesley hadn't wasted any time calling the police after Ollie woke up.

"Gena, if you were my sister or relative, I would take you to a safe place until the suspect is captured. He broke into a doctor's office early this morning and stole bandages, and a few boxes of sample painkillers. Our best guess is that he is going to try to set the wrist himself, rather than risk getting medical treatment by going to a hospital. We have people on their way to his residence, now that we know who we are looking for. I will wait here until we hear if they caught him or not. You're the only witness we have that has seen

his face. We have several samples of his DNA, but he's not in the system, so until we capture him we can't do much with the evidence."

This was not what she wanted to hear. They should have captured this guy last night, but now that he was still on the loose, she wondered how long it would be before he found a way to silence her. She looked around at the only real home she'd ever had. Her parents had been renting an apartment at the time of their deaths.

Ollie owned this condo. Her parents had given it to her when they moved to the small island country, Malta, where they had enjoyed the sun, and made new memories. Ollie had taken over the mortgage, paying it off within a few short years, thanks to the generosity of her male friends.

The elder Fullers had died last year in a boating accident. Ollie had been, understandably, devastated. Gena had been upset too, but since she couldn't remember ever meeting them, it didn't qualify as a big deal to her. She supported Ollie through the wake and the memorial service for her loved ones, but couldn't really understand what her cousin was going through. Sure, Gena had loved her parents, but they weren't a tight knit family.

Since the bodies had been burned, along with several others, and the boat sank, there had been nothing to bury.

Chapter 11

Gena reluctantly agreed to stay with Wesley and Ollie for a week, and Sergeant Mitchell asked if they minded if a female officer spent a few days in the condo. If the suspect was planning to come back to cause Gena harm, he would be met by a trained officer, or maybe two.

"It's highly unlikely that he will show his face anywhere near here. Yet, we can't discount the possibility that he might decide to eliminate a witness.

"We'll keep you updated if we find out anything." If she hadn't noticed the wedding ring on the handsome cop's finger, she would have sworn he was flirting with her.

She was a mess. Her recent activities with Trey and Quinn would be a hard act to follow for any one man. Plus, she was still pretty sure that she had fallen in love with the two men, and now wasn't the time for a rebound. Not that the cop was a viable candidate for a rebound. She would never screw around with a married man. No matter how good looking he might be, she was no home wrecker.

With any luck, the police would find Stuart what's-his-face, and her life could get back to normal.

She had plans to make. She could pick Wesley's brain about starting up a business,

and maybe, even where he thought would make a good location.

She went to her room to pack some clothing, and eyed the box. What if the officer decided to look through her drawers? She grabbed the box and put it into the suitcase. She wrapped the other vibe and butt plug in an old t-shirt, dropping the bundle into her case.

When she went to meet Wesley and Ollie in the living room, she handed Officer Mitchell her key.

"I just bought groceries, and there is plenty of junk food, so your officer is welcome to help herself. The milk is fresh, so she will be doing me a favor if she drinks it so it doesn't spoil." She had to pull her hand back from his clasp. He was staring at her as if he wanted to say something more, but instead he shook his head, and turned to hold the door open for them to leave.

Gena looked over her shoulder to see that the stern look was back in place on the officer's handsome face, and wondered what he was thinking about. She drove her car, following Wesley and Ollie to their house, that was situated in an affluent neighborhood.

She felt a moment of sadness. She and Ollie were all that was left of the two branches of their families. The big house, situated at the top center of the horseshoe driveway, would be a great place to raise a family. Hopefully they planned to have a large family. That way no one would be left alone if a disaster happened and people died. It was her worst fear, being left completely alone.

If she ever married, her husband had better be willing to have at least three, or four, children. As a single child, she'd had no one to play with, or to help with homework, or gossip with, or anything. It was a very lonely existence, and there was no way she would condemn a kid to that kind of loneliness unless there was a damn good reason.

She parked her car around the side of the house, and brought her own cases to the door. At least there wasn't a butler or housekeeper, that would be too hard to get used to.

Wesley took her suitcase, and led her to a room down the hall from the master suite. It was a beautiful room, but the lavender wasn't something she would have picked for herself. She turned to him and smiled appreciatively.

"Thank you so much for inviting me into your home. I'm sure I would've been fine at the condo, but I guess it's better to err on the side of caution."

"Gena, relax," Wes said, as he shot her a reassuring smile. "Ollie loves you, and I love her. If she had to worry about you alone in the condo, with a nutcase on the loose, she would make me move into the place with the two of you. No offense, but that place gives me the creeps when I walk in the door. Too many ghosts if you can understand that.

"Anyway, the housekeepers show up at six in the morning to clean, and get the coffee going first thing. Make yourself at home, and if you need anything, or need to talk, I'm usually around in the late afternoon." He looked toward the door, then back to her. "I hope having you here will keep Ollie so occupied that she will calm down, at least until we see the doctor." He left the room, leaving her to unpack her suitcase.

The bathroom was shared with the next bedroom, but since no one was currently occupying the other room, she wouldn't have to worry about the other door being locked, or walking in on someone else.

Ollie was waiting for her when she came down the stairs. The poor girl looked like she was going to start crying again, and Gena knew that if Ollie began to cry right this minute, she would join her. Her ability to maintain a happy mien was being tested this week. She forced a grin, and started to chatter.

"I almost got lost finding the stairs from my room. You need to give me the nickel tour around here. How big is this place anyway?"

Over the next few days, Gena kept as busy as she could. Keeping Ollie's spirits up was a full time job.

The day that Wesley took Ollie to the obstetrician, Gena escaped the confines of the beautiful house.

"I plan to drive around to see a couple of real estate agents, and find out if they have the kind of place I might want to invest in." She and Wesley had discussed her ideas for an upscale bar and grill several times over the past few days, so he was aware of her wish to get moving on her project.

She resented the way he had started to give her orders.

"I guess that will be fine as long as you stay away from the condo and your usual haunts. I spoke with Mitchell, and they're not any closer to finding the bastard than they were before. If you can hold back for a few days, I can call a friend of mine, and he can set up a few showings. It's not like you have to move on this right this minute, you know. I can loan you the money for the down payment, and you can use yours for startup cash." Before they walked out the door to go to the doctor's appointment, "I would feel a lot better if you would wait until I can go with you, Gena."

All he got was a polite, "Thanks, Wes, but I'm a big girl. I know what I'm looking for, and you have your own responsibilities to deal with right now. I'll be fine." She almost laughed when he scowled about her stubborn stance. "You and Ollie have a good time today, we have plans to redecorate the room next to yours next week. It will be perfect for a nursery, and it's going to cost you plenty of that money you're so eager to hand out."

Her day had gone from hopeful optimism, to complete shit. Of the four places she had visited that were for sale, only one was even remotely what she was looking for, and it wasn't sustaining itself. Gena didn't mind hard work, she could use a broom and paintbrush just as well as the next person. The problem was that the neighborhood was becoming run down, and there were several vacant buildings close by already. Buying the place would be a big mistake on her part, and she knew it. All in all, so far, her day was a waste of time.

Even lunch had been a disaster. How can a waitress confuse a turkey melt with a tuna melt? Not to mention her request for no lemon in her iced tea was ignored. The creepy looking man across the dining room that stared at her with a scowl on his face, just topped off her bad experience.

Officer Mitchell called as she was getting into her car, and asked her if she would be available for him to bring some packages by the house, that had arrived at the condo in the past three days. She made arrangements for him to meet her at Ollie's house.

Since she still had time before she needed to be there, she stopped at the mall and went inside. She needed some new clothing, but hadn't decided what to buy.

The bookstore lured her inside with its display of tantalizing book covers. Seeing cover after cover of half-naked men with oiled muscles, and interesting blurbs, kept her busy for a while. Seeing a book cover with a woman on her knees, her hands cuffed behind her back, pushed thoughts of the other romances from her mind. Without reading the blurb, she picked up that first book, then she found several others with covers showing a woman in a submissive pose, and one that showed a whip in a man's hand. At the checkout, the clerk grinned at her and commented on the simple cover of the man's hand.

"He was in here yesterday, I got him to sign a copy of this for me. Do you know, he's the most popular Dom in the city?" She leaned closer to whisper, "A couple of years ago, after his wife died during a robbery, they say he allowed two of the toughest Dommes around to scourge his back until he was a bloody mess. The people that watched it happen say that he groaned a few times, but other than that, he let them beat on his back until their arms wore out. I went to the club last week and what they said must be true. I saw the scars on his back myself." The clerk kept gossiping as she collected Gena's money. "If you like this book, he told me he has another that will be released before Christmas."

All the way back to the house, all she could think about was the man who had grieved so much, he had needed such an outlet for channeling his emotions.

Could he have found peace through such pain? People did strange things when they felt guilt or remorse. Maybe grief was one of those emotions that could be dealt with, with physical punishment. She promised herself that his book would be the first one she would read out of the six she'd purchased.

Officer Mitchell was waiting for her when she got to the house. He wasn't in his patrol car. Instead there was a beautiful, vintage, 1960's muscle car parked in front of the house. It was painted Candy Apple Red, had wide tires on the back, and had a short spoiler on the trunk. From the magazines she'd seen, and the little bird on the side, she was certain it was a Plymouth Road Runner.

She would love to be allowed to drive it. She loved old cars. It wasn't as though she'd gotten that love from her father, or an uncle, or even a teacher. Nope, there was no influence outside of seeing a 1966 Dodge Charger, that her neighbor used to own. She loved the sound of the motor when he started it up and revved the engine. That was before her parents died. She often wondered what had happened to that car. The man who owned it was older, and he had let her hang out in his garage, while he tinkered with the Charger. She'd listened to him rattle on about vehicles and motors. They used to go through his collection of muscle car books and magazines, that he'd stashed in his hideout, aka the garage.

His wife was a sweet woman, who seemed to tolerate the chubby teenager that wore baggy clothes, and was often greasier than her husband by the time they closed the garage doors at dinnertime.

To this day, she couldn't decide which car she would want to own. There were too many to choose from. Now there was one sitting right in front of her and she ignored the man, even as she admired his car.

"Officer Mitchell, if I had known this beauty was going to be here, I would have broken several speed limits to get back. She is gorgeous. Does she have the six-pack, positraction? Those can't be Mickey Thompson's on the back. Do they even make them anymore…?" She dropped the bag of books, dropping to her knees beside the front wheel well to see how much restoration had been done to the front clip.

There were no small rippled lines in the metal to bump the paint, and when she looked at the side of the car she could see nothing but a smooth finish.

"How did you restore her to such a…" She looked up at him and swallowed hard, momentarily loosing her train of thought. The intense look in his eyes, and his stance made her shiver. She lowered her eyes and got to her feet.

"Sorry about that, I love old muscle cars. There's something about them that makes me happy." He bent to grab her bag of books, picking up the two that had fallen out, and shoving them back into the bag.

Since this was her day for bad luck, one of those books was of the hand holding the whip, and the other was of a woman with her arms stretched overhead, cuffed together, hanging from an unseen hook in the ceiling. She was blindfolded, and the tied strip of leather behind her head hinted that she was gagged too.

He handed her the bag and opened the passenger door of his car. He picked up two small boxes from the seat, before closing the door with a sold thunk.

She unlocked the door to the house, leading the way inside.

"Would you like a drink or something? I'm going to get some tea, but I'm sure there is beer in the fridge."

He said tea would be fine, and she poured him a large glass. Was his visit more than just an official one? In street clothing he looked sexier than ever, not that she planned to get involved with him, but still a girl could look, right?

He was sitting in the chair behind her watching every move she made. It made her nervous. His size, while not as tall as Trey, or Quinn, for that matter, was still intimidating. She wasn't afraid of him, but she wanted to be. She wanted to be repulsed by him instead of attracted. What kind of woman was she? She had just spent a weekend with two of the most sexually dominant men in the world, and now, she found a married man attractive too? She needed to get a handle on her libido, or find a fuck buddy, as Ollie called a casual sex partner. It seemed when she finally took the plunge into carnal delights, she decided to enter it with gusto.

His, "Call me Adam," seemed to open the conversation and he got down to the reason for his visit. "Look, Gena, the packages are just an excuse for me to see you again. I know that you're under a bit of stress, but the truth of the matter is, that a friend of mine asked me to check in on you, and to see how you were doing until he gets back from Europe. Trey said you were a special lady, and he wanted to make sure you had someone to talk to since he and Quinn left you like they did." He grabbed her hand and pulled her back down in her seat when she started to jump up from the chair.

"They planned to be back within a few days, but there was an explosion at one of the manufacturing plants that they have partnerships in, and they had to take off in the middle of the night. Believe me, they would have been back to see you if that hadn't happened. Trey called me two days after they left your place, but I was too busy to stop over to see you. He said he had been trying to phone you, but all he got was a generic answering machine message. Let me tell you, he is none too happy with you about that little prank. I was at the station when I heard the dispatcher repeat your address, and remembered that I should have taken the time to stop by, before something like this happened."

She didn't know whether to be embarrassed or mad about this turn of events.

"They actually told you? Why didn't they just call me?" She wanted to throw up. This really was a shitty day. "Look, I appreciate your kindness, and if I need anything, I promise I will call you. I hope everything works out alright for Trey and Quinn, and that no one was injured in the explosion, but I think it's time for you to leave." She wanted to find a deep hole and crawl into it.

How could they just pass her off to another man after the things they'd shared? How could they have shared the knowledge that they had both had her sexually? Was he staring at her with hunger in his eyes?

She knew she couldn't look at him without lusting after him, and it had only made her slightly ashamed of herself before. Now she was sickened by her reactions to him. A married man, that thought she was an easy piece of ass, because his buddies had fucked her. Her wet panties mocked her as she tried to pull her arm from his grasp.

"Let me go. I'm a big girl, and I can take care of myself. Trey and Quinn don't have to worry about me at all, I'm fine. I fought off the guy that tried to attack me. I'm not as fragile as they seem to think I am." He wasn't letting go of her wrist, so she finally looked at him. She wanted him to leave so she could go to her room and cry. "Isn't your wife and kids waiting for you at home?" She deliberately used a snide tone, hoping he would give up and leave. Instead his jaw tightened and the next thing she knew, she was hauled up off her chair and over his knees.

"What the hell do you think you're doing? Let me go, before I start screaming the place down. Wes and Ollie will be back in a few minutes and he will have your ass." She tried to roll off his lap, getting a hard smack on her rear end for her efforts. The next thing she tried, was to draw one leg off his thigh and get her toes on the floor to help her push the rest of herself off him. That was less successful than the attempted roll. She found her ass burning from the rapid smacks before she could draw a breath to curse at him.

"Little girl, you have been trying my patience, and I am done being nice. From now on, if I tell you something, your response needs to be, yes sir. You will not take that snotty, bitchy tone with me again, or this sweet ass is going to be very sore by the time the boys get back here. Do you understand me?" His hand was now rubbing over the spots he'd just punished.

"Your Masters have asked that I babysit for them, to keep you out of trouble until they can collect you to take you home with them. Trey knows I won't hesitate to spank your ass, or put you in time out, if you refuse to act like a good sub until they get back. Then, you will be their problem, again." He helped her to stand.

"Now that we have that out of the way, I owe you an apology. I should have checked on you the day after Trey called. The truth is, that I was reluctant to get involved with our relationship again. After Sara died, well let's just say, things weren't the same for me. Trey and Quinn were able to move on, but I couldn't."

She wanted to yell at him. Tell him to go to hell. But when he spoke in those choppy sentences, and mentioned the woman, Sara, he'd choked on her name. That was the only thing that stopped her from tearing a verbal strip off his hide. He wasn't looking at her as if he wanted to fuck her any longer. No, now he looked, stunned? He shook his head and walked to the front door.

Before opening the door, he turned his head to look at her. The hard, tough, cop face was back, and she was pissed at herself for feeling any compassion earlier.

"From now on, until we catch the suspect, you will have someone with you at all times. No more joy riding, making yourself into a target. I'll be back later tonight to take you to dinner and we will talk. Be ready at seven, I don't like to be kept waiting."

The growl of the 383 V8 didn't send a thrill down her back as it normally would have, as Adam Mitchell drove away from the house. She was so confused, nothing would have fazed her right now. At least nothing that she could think of.

"Is there an emotion that I haven't been subjected to in the past few days? For goodness sake, Gena, what in the hell is the matter with you? You haven't been acting normal since the day before you set eyes on Trey and Quinn." She realized she'd been talking out loud, to herself, and shook her head. This had to stop. Tonight she would tell Officer Adam to leave her alone. The way she felt at this minute, she wanted nothing to do with any man. Even tall, broad shouldered, domineering types, with large hands, and the strange ability to make her panties wet with a smile.

She decided to take her purchases to her room, remembering to pick up the two small boxes on her way up the stairs. She'd no more than dumped them on her bed, when she heard voices carrying through the hallway from downstairs, and surmised that Ollie and Wes were home. Maybe they would have some good news. Something to distract her for a while. The thought of a little person joining their family was the best news she could imagine.

After confirming that they were, in fact, going to be parents in eight months, the thrill of window shopping for baby items, making plans for the future, and discussing whether or not they wanted more than one child, Ollie was worn out. When she would have stayed chattering at Gena about the baby, and their future plans, Wes shook his head, and sent his wife to take a nap.

He came back down the stairs to see Gena staring out of the window, and decided to talk to her about the call he'd taken last night from Quinn. If Gena was playing a game, she had better pick men that were easier to screw with. Trey, Quinn, and now maybe even Adam, had finally come out of their grief with a vengeance, and little Gena was right in the middle of it all. If he'd had an inkling of what had already happened between the two men and Gena before now, he knew it for a fact after talking to his friend. If Ollie was correct, and Gena was totally innocent before the past weekend, the girl was a fast learner.

Chapter 13

"Gena, you want to grab a couple of drinks and meet me in the den, please? I need to talk with you about a few things, and we'll be more comfortable in there." He didn't wait for her to answer. The girl was a born submissive, even if she did try to fight it at times. Ollie had tried to get her to go to the club with her a few times, but had stopped asking because Gena was too shy to go to a place like that.

He watched as she walked into the room, opening the beer bottle cap, before she handed it to him. She stood in front of him until he nodded his head, then took her tea, and sat across from him, waiting for him to speak. He'd been so wrapped up in his wife, that he hadn't actually observed Gena for any length of time before.

"We haven't actually had any time to get to know each other very well yet, so this week I hope to get to know you better." She smiled and nodded her head a little, before shocking the hell out of him when she started talking about buying a business in another state.

"I think I might take a week and fly to either California, or maybe, I'll go down South to visit a couple of states to see if I like them. The only place that I saw, that was even close to what I'm looking for, is in a bad area. A business needs working people to survive and thrive, but all the businesses around that property are abandoned, or going under, so I crossed that place off my list. If I want to get serious about owning a place, I'd better expand my search, and be willing to keep an open mind. That might mean a new state.

"Now that Ollie has her forever place, I need to find mine, you know? I promise I won't be one of those distant relatives that moves in, and stays until you want to hire a hitman to get rid of them." She kept the smile on her face, so he wouldn't know that moving away from Ollie was the last thing she wanted to do, but Ollie had found her place, and she couldn't stick around here much longer.

Instead of being happy that she planned to back out of the newlyweds lives, letting them enjoy each other without extended baggage, Wesley got mad at her. She should have known, and might have seen the red creeping up his thick neck, into his cheeks, if she hadn't been making her speech to his shoulder. She hadn't been able to look him in the eye, and act like it was okay for her to leave the only person in the world that gave a damn about her.

"That's not what I expected to hear from you, Gena. In fact, I am actually surprised that you would be so selfish. What? Now that your surrogate mommy is replacing you with a new baby, you plan to punish her by running away from home? That's real mature, you little bitch." He turned away, clenching his fists, and stomping to the window before turning back to her. "Do you think I don't know what happened between you, Trey, and Quinn that weekend? Do you think I can't see what you are doing to everyone around you?

"Bluntly put, your only relative in the world, up and gets married, so you decide to become like she used to be. Maybe if you're more like her, you can find your own happy ending? You really fucked up that plan with Quinn and Trey now didn't you? I've seen those men in action with a sub before. By the time they were through with the sub, male or female, I might add, the sub would have followed them into hell, crawling on broken glass for just one more taste of their brand of sex. The big surprise is that you didn't say anything about relocating in Wisconsin so you could be close to them. You know, in case they need a booty call. Or in their case, a dungeon call. I was going to warn you about them. Did you know they've been calling me every day since last Monday, demanding your phone number? I have avoided returning the calls. For some reason I was trying to protect you."

The disgusted look he was eyeing her with was just too much. She was in no emotional state for this. She stomped over to him, stopping about three feet away, before waving her finger at him as she set him straight.

"First, I would do anything for Ollie. Anything. Second, asshole, I planned to move on so I wouldn't be in the way around here. I hear people talk about relatives that never go away, they just stay sucking the life from married couples. I am trying to do you a favor and leave before you cringe every time you hear my voice. Ollie has looked out for me since I was fifteen years old, I would never willingly hurt her, but like you said, she is going to have someone else to take care of, and me hanging around here all the time will just add to her feelings of responsibility. She deserves every scrap of happiness that comes her way.

"As for this past weekend. You want blunt? Well here is blunt for you. Yes, Trey and Quinn spent their time with me. Yes, we had sex. Yes, they are bossy bastards that made me crave whatever they wanted to dish out. I never thought I would be the kind of woman that was like that. Being fucked by two men at the same time, was never in any fantasy, or dream, of mine. When they left on Monday morning, I never heard another word from them. I did get a package, the one that that broke-dick fucker used to get me to open the door with." She had to take a deep calming breath. Wesley had moved to his desk, he sat on the edge waiting for her to finish, but fuck that. She knew this would be the one time she could tell it all, and he would damn well listen.

"The icing on my day came in the form of a certain Officer of the law, who informed me that Trey and Quinn have asked him to take care of me. Whatever else he said after that escapes me. I was so mad, all I could hear was the fact those two, not only, had me crawling on my hands and knees, they were trying to pass me off onto someone else after they got what they wanted. They took what should have been a fond memory, and turned it into something so filthy. As though I would do all of that stuff with the next guy they sent. I feel like they think I'm some mindless fuck doll, or something. Do you really want someone with that kind of reputation to be hanging around here with your wife and baby? Especially when you entertain important clients?

"Adam Mitchell has ordered me to be ready to go out with him tonight. Ordered, as if he had every right to tell me what to do. He threatened to spank me again if I don't do as he says." She'd given him all of it. Now he would be happy she planned to move away.

When she looked up, Wes was frowning, while shaking his head back and forth.

When he reached for his phone, poked at the screen, and held the thing to his ear, she stood up to leave the room. The snap of his fingers, along with the scowl on his face had her sitting back down. She almost swallowed her tongue when she heard Wesley address Trey.

After the niceties had been taken care of, she flinched when he began talking about her. "I don't give a fuck what kind of shit storm you two have been dealing with, you need to straighten this out with Gena, or leave her the hell alone. Adam showed up and started ordering her around. She has no idea about the history you all shared with Sara. I plan to tell her what little I know in a few minutes, but right now, she feels like you are trying to pass her off onto the next guy." He listened for a few minutes, before looking over toward her.

"You should have told her that before you walked out the door, Trey. I'll give her your number. If she feels like calling you, she will. If she doesn't call, I expect you to back off, and that includes Adam too. Tell him she is not going anywhere with him tonight, or any other night, unless she wants to." After another few minutes of listening to the voice on the other end of the line, Wes concluded the call with, "I didn't fucking stutter, man. You boys figure it out between you, but she gets to decide what she wants to do." He pulled the phone away from his ear, ending the call, even though she could hear someone still talking on the other end.

She wouldn't let her eyes meet his. Her hands were clasped together in a death grip, and she was sitting on the edge of the settee. He remembered the first plot the women had hatched up, and knew that she was worried he would lose Trey and Quinn's business. For someone her age, with a college degree in business, no less, she was as naïve as an egg.

"Gena, look at me." She did, but slid her eyes sideways, until he repeated his request. "I said look at me. Not the desk. Not the window. Me. This is something you need to understand. I don't have a contract with their company yet.

We are still negotiating pricing, as well as, the viability of retooling one of our manufacturing lines to accommodate their needs. So stop worrying about me losing business just because I schooled those two dumbasses. I haven't gotten to where I am by kissing asses, and I certainly won't start with them.

"Now, let me give you a history lesson about them. Trey, Quinn, and Adam are good friends who met in grade school, or maybe it was junior high... I'm not sure, and I really don't care. The story goes that they screwed their way through college together, and that two of them, I'm not sure which two, are bi-sexual. They kicked around for a while separately, before they decided that they missed the old life of sharing sexual partners together.

"Trey found Sara in a BDSM club somewhere in Kentucky, of all places. He brought her into the circle, and she seemed to cement them all together. They had a marriage ceremony, of sorts, with Adam becoming her legal husband. I only saw them together maybe three times, so I can only tell you what I know. She seemed perfectly happy with her choices in life, and none of our circle concerned ourselves about their sex lives. She was a pretty woman, and she had the most beautiful posture a man could ask for in a sub or a wife.

"She died from a gunshot wound to the heart one night when she was out shopping with her mother. She'd stopped at a liquor store to buy something for their anniversary.

123

While she was paying for her purchases, the door opened and the shooting began. There were three hoodlums. They snatched the phone from her hand, and stomped it onto the tile floor. The police never solved the crime. Sara, and two other customers, were shot dead. The clerk behind the cash register lost an eye.

"They had been living just outside the city here. As far as I know, the place has been sold, and Adam is now a silent partner in the company that Trey and Quinn run. He decided to become a cop. I think he is still looking for the guys who killed Sara. The fact that she was buying the booze for the guys to tell them she was expecting a baby must have made it much worse. They didn't only lose Sara, they lost a baby, too."

Gena listened to the story, tears running unchecked down her cheeks. To have actually found men that loved her that much, and knowing a baby was on the way, it had to have been pure bliss for Sara. She felt sorry for the three men, especially when Wesley continued the tale.

"After the funeral, the guys moved to Wisconsin. Adam came back to Michigan within six months. He was their company lawyer, now he's a cop. I watched two Dommes beat that man bloody with whips one night at the club, and he never did more than flinch. He probably carries the scars to this day." He took a long pull off his forgotten beer, then scowled at the bottle. Damn the stuff was warm now, and tasted like horse piss, but his throat was dry so he drank it anyway.

"The fact that he busted your ass today is a surprise to me. He still goes to the club, but I never see him touch a sub. He'll discipline them. He'll teach them what it is to be a sub, but his hands are not involved when he does it. There are a few male slaves that hang around, and he does let them suck him off occasionally, but I haven't seen a woman get close to him since Sara."

*****

After the heart-to-heart talk, they moved into the kitchen, where Gena started to prepare dinner. He sat at the counter, watching her move around the kitchen. Trey had told him that they had plans for the girl, but he'd hung up on him before listening to anything more.

She was certainly worth a second, and even a third, glance. If he wasn't so hung up on his little, red headed wife, he would have tried to take her for a ride himself. From what he'd seen, Gena would be an asset to any man, let alone three men, who desperately needed an anchor.

Gena was the complete opposite of Sara in looks, and she wasn't as in your face either. Gena was blessed with large breasts and wide ass, whereas, Sara had been slender, and almost flat chested. Her ass was boyish, but her legs had been showstoppers, they'd seemed to go all the way to her neck.

However, the affair turned out, he would do his best to see that Gena was in good hands. Ollie would kill him if he didn't.

Chapter 14

Trey tossed his phone onto the table and stomped off to find Quinn. This entire week had been one fuck up after the other. It was time for them to dish out some tough love to these fuckers. It didn't seem to matter what his question to the manager of the manufacturing plant was, the guy just stood there trying to convince Trey that he didn't speak English. Since Trey had talked with the man on the phone numerous times in the past, he'd called him on it and now couldn't get a damn thing out of the man. Time to up the ante.

Quinn was helping sort out the rubble that was covering a CNC machine when he finally found him. He was sweating and tossing metal around like the Hulk himself. The only things missing were the green skin and giant status.

"Hey, when you get finished destroying the destruction here, come back to the hotel, we have things to discuss."

Quinn came into the small boarding house and immediately hit the shower. The physical work was a welcome change from standing around with his thumb up his ass, while Trey did his best to find out exactly what happened here. Maybe what he had found while unearthing the pricey Milling machine would shed some light on the subject.

The wiring in the place was mostly knob and tube, circa 1950's. Their partner had been mysteriously absent since they'd gotten here almost a week ago, so he was suspect number one as far as Quinn was concerned. They'd just spent a small fortune upgrading the electric and machinery. Obviously, the machinery couldn't have been substituted with old stuff since they had sent it from America. The big problem was that the electrical upgrades were supposed to have been completed before the multi-million dollars worth of equipment was set in place, and put into production. They had been lucky to get such a quick flight here. The day they'd arrived, there had been flatbed semi-trailers sitting next to the building ready to haul the new machines away for scrap, according to the shady looking guy who had tried to say he'd purchased them already.

He found Trey lying on the small couch, in the tiny sitting room provided by the boarding house with the cost of the room.

"Well, I can tell you that the machines weren't running when the fire started. In fact, according to Johnny, no one has been at the plant in a couple of weeks. The workers walked off the job because they weren't being paid. I searched through the mess, and found out the half million we allotted for the electrical upgrade hasn't been done.

"Looks like our pal Biscutte flew the coup with our money. With the building not being up to code, we will be damned lucky if the insurance covers the building. We also owe forty-two men and women paychecks for the last two weeks that they worked without pay." He rubbed his hands through his shaggy hair. "I don't know about you, but I'm ready to call in someone to deal with the recovery of the machinery, and to deal with these poor bastards that have been living hand to mouth since he skipped out on them."

Trey thought the shitty day couldn't get worse until he heard this.

He did something he rarely ever did, and made a snap decision. He hated calling someone else in to deal with this, but the only other option was to stick it out. They would have to relocate the manufacturing plant, and put new personnel in place, before going home to straighten everything out with Gena. Given the slow pace of anything done around here, that wasn't going to happen. He grabbed his phone and hit the icon next to Adam's name. He put it on speaker, setting the thing between him and Quinn's chair.

When Quinn gave him a quizzical look, he said, "Wait a minute, I don't want to repeat this over again."

Adam must have been sleeping because he sounded groggy when he answered the phone. "Are you awake enough to talk?" At his grumbled affirmative answer Trey outlined the entire deal with Gena. "I texted you earlier so you wouldn't go over to pick her up and have Wes meet you with a shotgun. He is more protective of the girl than most fathers are. He called me this morning, and lit into me over her. I told him this was an emergency and that we'd tried to call, but no one answers the damn phone. I didn't tell him about the stuff we have been mailing to her, it's not his business.

"Bottom line, she thinks we fucked her for fun, then sent you over to take seconds. He didn't say it, but she probably thinks that when you're done you will try to pass her on to the next guy. I told him we said we'd be back, and that we have tried every day to call her. He says to get our shit together and decide what we want. He's going to give her my number. If she wants to call, she will."

Quinn listened to the cursing coming through the airwaves. He was mentally doing some cursing himself. It had been two years since they'd all been together. Two long fucking years. Now that they'd found Gena, it was like there was a reason to smile again for no reason. Letting that feeling go wasn't going to be allowed. He opened his mouth to voice his opinion, but Adam's news hit him like a sledgehammer.

"She was attacked by a guy that has been preying on single women in the apartment and condo communities. She was number five, but he got more than he bargained for with her. She broke his fucking wrist, and she wasn't about to feel bad about it either. I had already been after this fucker, but she not only broke his wrist, she identified him. Well, she saw him, her cousin actually gave us his name, but Gena sketched a very close picture of the assailant. I think she's more mad than scared. She's staying with Wes and Olivia. She's the only victim who has seen his face. She can identify him, and he knows it. The phone is still in her cousin's name, so when she kept getting hang up calls she turned it off. That's why you haven't had any luck getting her on the phone."

Quinn broke into the conversation, he wanted answers, and wanted to be on a plane back to the States. "How did she break his wrist? Did he hurt her? Why haven't you caught the motherfucker? You keep her little ass safe. Do you hear me, Adam? One or both of us will be home by the end of the week."

He heard Adam's, "Yeah, I heard you, I'm not deaf."

"Look, I don't know how you feel about her, and I know it's not exactly rational of me to be so hung up on her, but I actually really like her. I think she's one of those rare forever type of women. I want that, for all of us. Not to open healing scars here, but she is nothing like Sara was. I loved Sara as much as any of us did. But, unlike you, I'm not willing to lie down in that cold grave with her.

"I want another shot at happiness, and I believe Gena could give us that. I want a home, kids, the whole fucking package. I want you guys to be there with me, but if you want something else that's fine too. Let's put our cards on the fucking table here. You have my vote, now you need to ask yourselves what you want." He stood and headed for the door.

Trey asked him where he was going. He wasn't at all surprised with Quinn's answer.

"I'm going to do what has to be done, so that I can get on a plane, get back to Michigan, and try to fix this fucking mess we are in with Gena."

Trey knew Quinn was going to get shit done now. When Quinn was in this kind of mood, it was best to just stand back and let him go for it. He had other things to do. Like deal with the local authorities, and pay the former employees that had been victims of their absent partner.

"All right, Adam, if you see her, tell her we will be coming for her as soon as we can get away. Try to explain what's going on, and for God's sake, keep her safe. I don't know about you, but I lean toward Quinn's assessment of our lives. I'm tired of looking for something that isn't there. To tell you the truth, when I first set eyes on the girl, I wanted her. She's not sweet tempered, or trained, and for a virgin she was more enthusiastic than I'd dreamed possible. The palm of my hand fit her butt cheek like it had been designed for me to spank. I swear she sassed me just so I would feel the need to paddle her ass."

Adam was laughing as he told Trey about his experience with Gena.

"I noticed her mouth first thing, man. I could see it wrapped around my prick. I ended up spanking her too, and after a token resistance, she was creaming so much I could smell her scent. I threatened her with another spanking if she wasn't ready when I came to pick her up, but we both know how that ended, so yeah, I owe her a good one on that beautiful ass."

They talked for a while longer and formulated a plan of action. Adam was going house shopping, and would arrange for furnishings. He would also get their stuff out of storage. Ten days wasn't much time to get everything done. He would need to throw some money around to obtain a suitable house within their target date, but he was confident that he could do it. When he'd finished his call with Trey, he made another one, this time to Quinn.

Quinn answered the phone, with a cautious, "Yes?"

Adam, for the first time in two years, just started talking. He told Quinn that when Sara had been killed, he'd not only stopped living his normal life, he'd cut Quinn from his life too. As if he was doing penance for the crime of enjoying the close relationship the two men shared. They'd been lovers, as well as, friends, and Adam had abandoned him. He'd taken all of the warmth and love that they'd shared when he left. He had punished himself, but he'd punished Quinn too. He owed the man. Owed him more than the shitty way he'd been treating him, that was for sure.

"I want you to know that I agree with you. Gena seems to be exactly what we need. I know that I've been a selfish prick. Hell, man, there hasn't been a day that's gone by that I haven't missed you guys. Especially you. I just didn't know how to fix my fuck up. Let's face it, I have never been able to tell people that I care about them without my nuts being squeezed in a vise. One more point in the girl's favor, she's given me the excuse I've needed to apologize, and maybe repair some of the damage I've caused to you, and to Trey." He waited for a few tense seconds. Quinn acted like such a badass most of the time, that no one that met him would know he was actually a very kind man. A man with feelings. He had so much love to give. It humbled Adam to be part of this man's life, his inner circle, and he was ashamed that he'd removed the comfort of his own love for Quinn and Trey. It was past time to man up. He was going to grab this possible second chance at happiness.

*****

Quinn stood with his back to the sizzling hot metal siding of the ruined building, as he listened to Adam tell him that he was sorry for abandoning them. He knew it took a lot for the man to voice an apology. Could he forgive him? Forget the way he'd crawled away, swearing allegiance to Sara's ghost, and vowing vengeance on those responsible. He'd barely said goodbye.

No, this was not the time to make that type of decision. There was just too much to

134

discuss, and an overseas phone call wasn't the way to do it.

Taking a deep breath, Quinn said, "When I get back, we can talk. We have to get the air clean between us if there is any hope of a happy ending to this. I meant what I said. I want it all. I'm not going to settle for little pieces of a life again. No more fucking hiding. No more pretending that I have a separate social life outside of our relationship. Trey knows how I feel about this, and he agrees with me. So you need to think about that too." He ended the call, without waiting for a response from Adam. He had things to do, and with the mood he was in, well, it was probably a good thing Biscutte was still MIA. He yelled for Johnny.

"Okay, buddy, here's the deal. You go and find me as many strong men as you can get. I also need you to find a couple of nice ladies who like to cook, and then get back here at first light. Tell the people we will pay them each day, and the ones that are owed money will be getting checks for the past month. Two of those weeks are for money owed to them, and the rest is severance to help tide them over until we can get this place up and running again. If you, or anyone else, knows of a large building that we can temporarily set up business in until a new building can be constructed, bring me an address. Trey can check it out. We want this mess cleaned up by the end of the week, so we need a place for this machinery as soon as possible."

Instead of waiting around for help to come, or wait for the crew Johnny would be bringing in the morning, Quinn started hauling more scrap from the building. At home he would hit the gym. Here, physical labor was his answer to dealing with the turmoil inside his guts.

Chapter 15

Ollie was puking her guts up in the bathroom, while Wes held her long red hair out of the way, and Gena brewed ginger tea to soothe her cousin's poor tummy.

When the doorbell sounded over the sounds of retching, Gena hurried to the door and, without looking to see who it might be, opened the door. As soon as she turned the handle and started to pull it open, it was pushed inwards with a lot of force. She barely got out of the way of the door without being knocked down.

Her breath caught in her throat when she saw Stuart standing in the doorway with an odd looking gun in his hand. It was boxy, with bright yellow coloring at the end of the barrel. The man looked like hell. His face was red and puffy. He had a dirty bandage holding his broken wrist straight, and his hand was stained with something nasty looking. The fingers that were visible over the bandaging were purple and swollen, like purple fingerling potatoes. If he wasn't holding a stun gun on her, she might have offered to help him. As it was, she was mad at herself for opening the door without looking.

"I finally found you, bitch. You thought you could hide, didn't you? Fuckin' tramp." He waved the gun in his own direction to emphasize his next point, as Gena saw Wesley coming toward them from the hallway behind the wide open door. She wanted to warn him about the idiot with the gun in his hand, but Stuart's voice was loud enough to wake the dead, so she was sure Wes could hear the psychopath.

"I am a cyber fuckin' genius. No one can hide from me. You thought I would give the fuck up, right? Hahahaha, now I gotta kill you, so I can go back to my place without the cops being able to pin a damn thing on me. You couldn't have just let me fuck you, could you? I noticed the way you got round heels for those two big motherfuckers on Sunday. The least you could have done was let me have some fun. You would be none the worse for wear. I mean maybe you'd have a few bruises, and a sore cunt, but I would have let you live. Now I don't have a choice. You gotta die."

While Gena was trying to decide what to do, Wes had heard the last of this guy's threats, and was reaching for the door when she saw someone tackle the unsteady man in front of her.

The two men landed at her feet. Her assailant was screaming, and trying to roll out from under Adam, but he wasn't getting anywhere. The man stopped screaming when Adam slapped the back of his head into the tiled floor.

"Shut up, asshole. You're hurting my ears. You like hearing women scream when you hurt them, you should love what I'm doing here." Adam pulled the man's injured arm from under him, and tsked at the way it flopped when he dropped it next to Stuart's head. "I bet what I'm doing makes you think I'm a big ol' pussy, don't you? I'd like nothing better than to make you scream 'till you can't scream again, but I have rules to follow," Adam read Stuart his Miranda rights, before lowering his voice.

"Understand this, jackass, I can't give you what you deserve, which is a bullet, but I can give you a nice cozy jail cell. You'll even get a doctor to work on that wrist. And for you, I'm going to be kind and tell the doc that you like pain, so he won't have to worry about hurting you too much. Now be a good little bitch, there's a car coming to pick you up."

Adam called for a patrol car to come get Stuart and take him for medical treatment, then to jail. He picked up the weapon, examining it, before he started laughing at the man lying under his knee. "You dumb shit, you should know your weapon before you try something so fucking stupid. There's no batteries in it."

Wes let the patrolmen in the door. He waited until they had hauled Stuart out, before shaking his head at Gena. He completely ignored Adam, and began to lecture her on proper security practices. She sat there, listening to his rant, because she'd known better. Even though she hadn't done it on purpose, it was still a stupid mistake.

"I'm sorry, Wes. I really didn't even think. I ran to get the door, because you were busy helping Ollie. I had the kettle on, ready to make tea for her-" She remembered the kettle was still on the stove and jumped up, running into the kitchen to turn the burner off.

The men followed her, watching as she poured the last of the water into a mug, before adding the spicy ginger, chamomile tea bag. She added a teaspoon of sugar and set it in front of Wesley. "This should help with the nausea."

*****

She smiled at Adam, and thanked him. Then she turned away, pulling the door under the sink open to remove a small, red bucket and a large yellow sponge. She placed the items in the sink, then walked into the laundry room off the kitchen, coming back with a bottle of bleach. She poured a generous amount into the bucket, before turning on the hot water to fill it.

Adam watched her as she worked. Anyone looking at her would think she was unaffected by the recent events in the foyer. However, he could see the rapid blinking of her beautiful green eyes, and the slight trembling in her hands as she tried to keep busy. She turned off the water, ducking back down under the sink for a pair of green rubber gloves. She pulled them on, grabbed the bucket and sponge, and walked into the foyer.

Both men followed her path. Wesley skirted around her with the mug of tea to give it to Ollie, while Adam watched Gena survey the smeared bloodstains on the tiles. She dropped to her knees, and began cleaning up the mess. Once the entire area was clean, she kept scrubbing with the sponge, pushing it harder and harder until Adam stepped close and pulled her to her feet. He took the sponge, and pulled the rubber gloves off her hands, dropping them into the bucket, before taking her trembling body into his arms, holding her tightly to his chest.

It felt right. She felt right. For the first time in over two years he had a woman in his grasp. A woman that needed his strength. A woman that he'd been lucky enough to save. The ice surrounding his heart was melting fast. When she started to pull away he gave her a quick squeeze, wanting to keep her close, but he let her go. He held her shoulders, giving her a small shake to get her to look at him.

"No one was hurt. The bad guy is in custody, and we can all sleep like babies tonight. Do you understand that? You're safe now." She wasn't crying, but her jaw was clenched, and those beautiful green eyes were shiny with unshed tears. She nodded her head at his words, before she looked back down.

She took a deep breath, reached her hands up, and grabbed his head to pull him down, holding him in place for the kiss she planted on his lips. He knew the kiss was to express her thanks for his intervention with Stuart, but he wished the kiss was for more personal reasons. She drew back and took her hands from him.

"Thank you for protecting me, and for arresting him, and for the comfort. I know I haven't exactly been the nicest woman to you, but I do appreciate your help." She bent to pick up the bucket, then headed into the kitchen, while he followed. The bucket went into one side of the sink, and she scrubbed her hands until they were pink. "I haven't had anyone tell me they planned to rape and kill me before. It's a bit unsettling. I guess as a cop you see this kind of thing every other day, right?"

He nodded noncommittedly. He didn't want to talk about his job. He had other things he needed to discuss with her. Unfortunately, he couldn't really talk to her here. Wes's home wasn't an ideal place to tell her about Trey and Quinn's plans, or to discuss his own involvement in the situation, for that matter.

Will you let me take you to dinner this evening?" He wanted to tell her he was taking her to dinner, then back to his place for a little training session, but he knew better than to take that tone with her yet. Wesley was *not* a man to make idle threats. The last thing he needed was for Wes to kick him out. If that happened, chances of a third shot at getting Gena to listen would be almost nil. "We'll go pig out on greasy burgers and fries. If you bat your eyelashes and giggle, I might even throw in a chocolate shake." He wiggled his eyebrows when he said that and sure enough, she giggled.

"Okay, dinner it is, but I want my chocolate shake." She walked him to the door. "Thank you again. I'll see you at six?"

*****

He left, and as she shut the door behind him, she noticed Wes standing in the hallway leaning against the wall. She expected him to voice an objection to her dinner plans, instead he just nodded his head as he turned around, heading back to his room.

Gena went back into the kitchen. Ollie would be hungry soon. As far as she knew, no one had eaten breakfast, or lunch, yet. It was a good thing actually, since when she was nervous, she cooked. Cooking the grilled chicken breasts, that were marinated in her own recipe, kept her busy. Angel hair pasta tossed in olive oil and garlic, sprinkled with a pinch of oregano, and crustini spread with olive oil and just the hint of garlic, completed lunch. She would have added a small salad to the meal, but Ollie couldn't look at a tomato without being sick to her stomach, so she omitted that from the meal.

Rather than yell that food was on the table, she texted Ollie's phone to let them know that lunch was ready. If they didn't come out of the room, she would put plastic wrap over the beautiful meal, so that they would have something to eat later.

She ate alone, after waiting twenty minutes. She planned to pack her stuff tonight, and go back to the condo tomorrow. She wanted to get back to the research she needed to do, but the thought of her date tonight overshadowed just about everything else. Adam was a handsome man, but so were Trey and Quinn. How could one woman keep the interest of three men? Even if two of them were bi-sexual, the numbers didn't add up, unless... Oh boy. Would all three of them want to have sex with her every time? That might get to be too much for her. She had to smile when the thoughts kept trolling across her brain. If she was going to be exhausted, there were worse reasons for fatigue.

She spent the afternoon doing laundry and repacking her bags. At two o'clock, Ollie strolled into her room and hugged her tight.

"I'm sorry for everything that you've been through. I feel responsible, for all of it, not just Stuart..." Ollie says, while still holding her.

Obviously, Wesley had been gossiping.

"Stuart was a fluke. Definitely not something that you could have ever seen coming," Gena sat down on one of the stools, that were around the island. She steered Ollie into the one next to her.

"And, if I'm right, Wes told you about the guys? All of them?" At Ollie's nod, Gena took a deep breath, and nodded. "Okay. The thing is, I don't know. I still have to decide if I want *all* of that. I don't even know where *they* stand, yet.

They are all wonderful guys, even if they're bossy," she grins.

"My big problem is, is that they have history together. A *lot* of history," she shrugs, and shakes her head. "I'm not ready to jump into anything like they had with their wife. Did Wesley tell you about that?" Ollie just nods, letting Gena do all the talking. "Not until I'm very, very sure that it's what I want," she grinned at her cousin. "If nothing else comes out of this, at least I've learned a few things about myself. Oh, and Ollie, wait until you see Trey and Quinn. They are every bit as hot as Adam Mitchell is."

Chapter 16

Adam came to get her in his Road Runner. He confirmed that it did indeed have a six-pack on a 440 cu ft engine. "Positraction rear end, and the wheels are vintage Craigers. Tell me again how you know all of this about a car that was built before you were born?"

She told him about the long suffering neighbor. She didn't realize that she was describing a childhood filled with emotional neglect. When a kid had to depend on a neighbor for emotional support, because she didn't get any from her parents, it left scars. "I spent hundreds of hours reading about muscle cars."

When he expressed sympathy concerning her parent's deaths, she shrugged.

"I was lucky that Ollie wanted me. Not every girl in her early twenties would take on a fifteen-year-old bookworm. Ollie has always been great. She's my best friend, more like a big sister than a distant cousin. I would do anything for her."

Adam ordered their meal, as Gena stood next to him trying to keep her mouth shut, but not succeeding.

"Adam, I might be a bigger woman than what you normally date, but there is no way I can eat one of those double cheeseburgers with everything and fries too. Really, you should change the order." He shook his head no, directing them to a corner booth.

Before she knew what he was doing, he'd dropped the tray on the table and crowded in next to her on the bench seat.

He leaned over and whispered in her ear, "The fact that you are larger than some women is a point in your favor, but I have another reason for ordering you the sandwich. I am banking on the fact that you will only be able to eat two thirds of that burger, if that. That leaves me the rest. Two of these burgers are too much, but one and a quarter fills my hollow legs, and makes me a happy boy."

He'd predicted her intake of the meal almost on the nose, and they shared a laugh about that. When they left the burger joint, he drove them to the condo to talk.

"I'm not about to have this discussion in front of other people. What we discuss is our business, no one else's. I would take you home to my place, but the maid hasn't been there in weeks, and there are piles of takeout cartons are everywhere. I figure you'll be more at ease at your place... So here it is."

Once they were inside the condo, seated in the living area, he began to talk. She was anxious to hear what he had to say, but more than that, she had a ton of questions.

"Why do the three of you want only one woman between you? I'm not that savvy about these things, but it seems strange to me that three healthy males want just one woman."

He patiently explained, "I don't know how to answer your question, other than to say that the three of us are closer than most brothers. I love those two meatheads and they feel the same way about me. Quinn and I have a special relationship. At the risk of scaring you away, we have shared a sexual relationship since junior high school. As we got older, we realized that we were also attracted to women. Trey was always our friend. He has a sadistic streak, and I like nothing better than to have my ass and back whipped while I top Quinn. When he tops me, Trey often directs the play. The closest he wants to be to another man's prick is when we are both inside a woman and can feel each other through the membrane that separates her vagina and ass. That is some good friction.

"I love seeing a woman's mouth wrapped around my cock, while watching Trey or Quinn fuck her at the same time. It's fucking hot." He got very quiet for a few moments, then said, "When Sara died, I let both of them down. I had married her so she would have the protection of my family name, and she made us draw straws to see which of us would be Mr. Sara. I felt so guilty that one of us hadn't been there to protect her the day she died, that I went a little crazy. I quit practicing law, moved away from the only real comfort I could have had, and did everything I could think of to atone for her death.

"I have been cautioned by the Chief of Police to be nicer to domestic abusers. I was almost involved in a lawsuit for abusing a guy that beat his wife to death, their baby was found sitting in his mother's blood, screaming his little head off. When we got there, the fucker was standing over her dead body, yelling at her to get her lazy ass up and fix his dinner. I took him out and beat the shit out of him before backup arrived, while my partner got the baby away from the mess. I kept seeing Sara in the woman lying on the floor. I was the only one that knew she was pregnant at the time, that little boy just brought it home to me how much I- I mean we, lost that day. I ended up taking two weeks off, and tried to find some outlet for my pain.

"One night, I decided that I was finished with it. I was going to stop hurting and paying for something I had no control over. I went to the club, assessed the people there, and found two Dommes that knew how to wield a wicked whip. I had a safe word, and they were told not to stop until I used it." He looked away, then back to her. "After the first ten minutes I didn't feel a thing. I have to hand it to those women, they knew what they were doing. I was so far gone, I was not about to stop them. What they did for me that night was the best feeling I'd had in all the time since Sara died. They stopped when my back was a bloody mass of flesh. I told them to continue, but they refused.

"The beauty of not feeling, not hurting, no guilt, all of it gone, was a heady feeling. I guess I laughed like a lunatic afterwards, while they cleaned me up and put medication on my wounds. The patrons that night could be forgiven if they walked out with the impression I was some kind of pain slut, or worse. Since that night, I feel lighter in my soul. It didn't purge her from my heart, but it's made life more bearable.

"I haven't had sex with a woman since Sara, and it shocked me that when I saw you, all I wanted to do was lay you down and bury myself in your body. Imagine my surprise, when it finally registered, that you were the one Trey called me about to look in on." He sat deeper in the thick cushions and ran his fingers through his short brown hair.

Wow, this man had certainly laid his past open to her... She knew parts of it already, thanks to Wesley. And it hadn't taken a lot of imagination to figure out who had written the book the salesgirl had discussed with her. He had seen she bought the book the day she discovered his car in the driveway.

"Can I ask you a few questions?" At his nod, she surprised him by asking, "Is it odd that I like being spanked? I liked almost everything Trey and Quinn did that weekend. I even liked it when they acted all bossy and dominant. Even when something hurt, I loved it, and begged for more. Is that normal?"

"If you liked it, it's normal. Some people like a bit of bite to their lovemaking. You just happen to be one of them. I'll tell you right now, if we can all work on a relationship together, you will be paddled often. I already owe you a good, bare assed spanking. It's taking a lot of willpower to sit here without baring your ass, and giving it to you right this minute." He stood and came to sit next to her on the couch.

"How will I know that this will work out for all of us? I may be young and dumb, as they say, but how do you know? I opened the two packages that you brought to me the other day and I almost peed my pants when I saw what was in them. Did you know that there was a silver choker and a very pretty set of silver hoop earrings in one box, and in the other was three DVDs. I haven't watched them yet. Everything has been happening so fast, but my heart thumps every time I see the boxes in my drawer."

He wanted to laugh at her bewildered look. She was genuine in her concern about the dynamics of an arrangement like he and his friends were proposing.

"I'll make a deal with you. You said that you're moving back here tomorrow? How about I come by when my shift is over and you can fix dinner for us. We can watch the DVDs together. That way if you have any questions, I will be right here to answer them. Does that sound like an acceptable plan to you?"

She nodded and smiled. This could work out. Living with Ollie was an eye opening experience, but the thought of doing half of what these men were proposing made her breathe deeply.

"Now, let's get you back to the house before good old Wes sends out a search party for you."

He dropped her off, walked her to the door, and proceeded to kiss the hell out of her. Like full frontal touching, back against the door, breathtaking, kissing. Adam didn't make any effort to hide the thick hard-on pushing into her belly. He tore his mouth away from hers, resting his head beside hers as he steadied his breathing.

"I will see you tomorrow night around six-thirty. We can talk more." He turned the handle opening the door before pushing her through it and pulling it closed. Within seconds she heard the throaty growl of his car, and smiled to herself.

She still wasn't sold on the idea of three men, but at least it wasn't as bad as she'd first thought. She had a lot to think about. For now, she decided to keep an open mind and hope she made the right decisions.

She saw that there was a light on in the kitchen, so she headed that way to see if the food she'd left had been eaten yet. She found Ollie in the kitchen, with her ass in the air, as she rummaged through the fridge. The dirty dishes in the sink showed her that at some point the newlyweds had indeed eaten the meal she'd left for them. It took a couple of minutes for the mother-to-be to emerge with an armful of deli meat, cheese, and condiments.

Ollie looked like she had discovered a pot of gold, as she lovingly gazed at a jar of jalapenos she snagged just before the fridge door shut.

Gena asked, "Do you need some help there?" Although the redhead froze for a moment, she shook her head and dropped her bounty on the center island. She then proceeded to assemble the largest sandwich known to mankind.

"How'd it go? Is he as hot in bed as he looks like he would be?" Ollie was munching on the jalapenos, while cramming the thick sandwich into her mouth as if she hadn't eaten for the entire day. Seeing her thin cheeks puffed out with food, while she tried to talk, made Gena smile. She looked like a freckled chipmunk.

"I don't know how hot in bed he is… Yet. He is sexy though, isn't he? I can tell you he knows how to kiss a girl, and if the hard-on that was pressed into my stomach when he pinned me to the door is any indication, he has all the right equipment to make a girl smile."

Gena made them each a cup of cocoa, while they sat discussing the attributes of men and sex. She was shocked when Ollie opened up, finally telling her about her hang-ups and former professional rules.

"I had a friend in grade school, her name was Bailey. We were best friends until her uncle molested and raped her. She confided in me about it, and I told my mom, who in turn called the police. Bailey caught all kinds of hell from her family for telling on her uncle. They treated her like it was her fault, as if she had lured him into stuffing his prick into a kid. I heard her mother call her a slut, among the nicer insults that she spewed.

"She was only ten years old when her grandmother called her a whore, and told Bailey that she would never get a decent man to marry her since she was no longer a virgin. When she was eleven-" Ollie choked a bit on her words. "When she was eleven, she killed herself. She walked in front of a semi-truck. We were standing at the corner, and she had just told me that her uncle had only gotten probation for ruining her life.

"Traffic was heavy, and we had been waiting a while for a break to cross the road. She turned her head to me, said goodbye, and stepped right into the road. She did it on purpose, I know she did. She was smiling when she stepped off that curb, tears were falling down her cheeks, and she smiled at me. She found her solution, her way out of an intolerable situation. A year later the uncle was arrested again for molesting one of the girls in the neighborhood, and even after everything that had happened with Bailey, those people were telling everyone in the grocery store the girl was a little slut. It came out in court that he had been molesting little girls for years, but the families were old world types from overseas, and the female was always blamed for luring men into fucking them. The uncle was killed in prison."

She sipped her cocoa and stopped talking for a few minutes. "I never realized how fucked up I was until you were in college. I actually went to a psychiatrist for three years, before I finally figured out that I was keeping my hymen to avoid being labeled a slut. All that time, all those men, and I was still fucked in the head over what happened almost twenty years in the past. Any man that called me a slut never got a repeat date.

"When Wesley came along, I made up my mind that things would be different. I wanted to be a normal, healthy woman, not some kinky bitch with a string of ex-lovers and childhood hang-ups. I wanted to be a whole person with him. *For* him. I wanted to be proud of myself, and when he didn't turn around at the door and leave after I told him about my past," She shook her head, before taking a deep cleansing breath. "He says he saw something worth sticking around for. I thank God that he did." She grinned and wiggled her eyebrows. "He even gives me spankings when I push his temper. Can you imagine that? Me, pushing him into paddling my naughty butt?"

They shared a laugh over that. It had never been a secret how much Ollie loved a good spanking. Over the years, she had frequently had trouble sitting the morning after having her ass wailed on by an enthusiastic date. Many times Gena had fetched a pillow from the couch so that Ollie could be, somewhat, comfortable sitting on one of the hard wooden chairs at the kitchen table.

"So, now that I've spilled all of my darkest secrets, it's your turn. Tell me about the men you've gotten involved with. I want details. I want to know everything."

By the time Gena had told her everything she was willing to share, she was tired. Ollie had interrupted the recounting of her newfound sexual exploits with numerous questions and demands for clarification. One time, she'd even had to stop talking, so her cousin could run to the bathroom. Gena changed their drinks to herbal tea while waiting for her to get back. For the first time ever, Gena had rendered Ollie speechless for a full five minutes.

Chapter 17

The first DVD was one on submissive behavior. Gena wondered who had come up with the rules, until the narrator speculated that ancient writings and hieroglyphics depicted slaves, or in the case of a submissive, calm creatures waiting on their knees with hands palm up to show there was no task they would refuse. Ancient tombs of character behavior and practices had been adapted for more modern times.

Adam had her mimic the poses, then slipped a leather collar around her neck while she was on her elbows and knees, trying to get the curved angle to her back that the submissive on the screen was displaying. His compliment of "beautiful" was not meant for the graceful pose. He had been staring at the leather neck gear when he said it. Moments later he'd given her the order to strip out of her clothing for better ease of movement.

"Trust is the most important emotion between you and your Dominant. In this case Dominants. Trust me when I say you'll be happy that you are naked for this next show. While you're at it, bring your toys that the guys gave you. We will go over the use of toys that are used for pleasure, and punishment." He had a wicked gleam in his eyes that she wasn't sure she liked, but they had already gone this far. Hell, her panties had been soaked since the minute he'd told her to go to her knees. She shivered in anticipation of what was about to happen.

She'd slipped into the bathroom to wash her soaked thighs and crotch. The slippery juice kept sliding from her body as she ran the damp cloth between her legs, so she did the best she could to dry herself off, then slipped into clean panties, before gathering her toys.

She came back into the room blushing, with her arms full of the small collection of toys.

Adam was placing a kitchen chair where the coffee table had been, and a laptop was open to the side of the TV. The split screen picture showed Trey and Quinn on a side by side conversation with Adam.

Trey saw her first and smiled, "There she is."

Quinn just grinned at her, nodding his head in greeting. Adam took the arm full of toys, and pulled the thin robe from her shoulders. She stood there in her bra and panties and nothing else. Adam frowned at her, and asked why she was wearing clothes.

"I thought that this was okay," was apparently the wrong answer.

He snapped his fingers at her and she dropped her head, removing the skimpy pieces of cloth quickly. She heard Trey order her to look at them. When she looked up he twirled his finger in a motion indicating she should turn around so the men could see all of her. She

complied, having to stop herself from crossing her arms in front of her.

Adam sat in the hard chair. He pulled her down onto his lap, facing the computer screen. He draped each of her legs over his thighs, spreading his own as far as possible. In this position she was wide open for the men watching. They nodded in approval, their expressions ones of undisguised lust.

Adam pulled her nipples away from her body, steadily increasing the pressure as he pinched the chubby nubs. Something snapped inside of her. She arched, trying to increase the pressure. The bite of nipple clamps made her pull back for a moment, the slight pain making her squeal, while even more liquid flowed between her legs.

The slap of his broad hand on her labia and clit, brought tears to her eyes, but she shuddered as another part of her rejoiced at the sting of discipline. The next four smacks progressed in intensity. She would have begged him for more if he hadn't taken her clit between his fingers, giving it a hard pinch. She screamed, wishing his fingers would slip up and push into her needy body.

Whatever Quinn said was lost on her as she begged Adam to do something, anything to relieve the pressure that was fast building. She wanted him to move his fingers just a bit more, she even tried to buck her hips up, but all she got was another slap on the wetness between her thighs.

159

"You don't come until one of us says you can, that's the rule. Now, I want you to bend forward until your hands touch the floor, then rest your head on your hands." She hesitated, trying to figure out how to comply with the order. Adam pushed her shoulders forward to help her.

"I've got your legs, you won't fall," was whispered into her ear, as she did her best not to panic. Her hands landed hard, but she was no longer afraid since she felt the firm floor under her palms. Adam pulled her thighs higher onto his lap, and received compliments on his technique.

"Very nice, I can see her little pucker from here. Damn, that's pretty. From the amount of wetness, I see, she isn't against a pussy spanking either. Isn't that right, Regina?" She nodded her head, getting a slap on the ass for not answering him verbally. "When you're asked a question, you will answer with words. Do you understand?"

Her, "Yes, Sir," was the right answer, and she relaxed a little bit. Adam was petting her ass, and sliding his fingers from one end of her slit to the other, stopping along the way to tweak her clit, and stick a long finger into her cunt. She squealed again when he suddenly pushed a finger into her anus. Pushing herself upright shoved his finger deeper and she cried out. It seemed each time she moved, the clamps on her nipples banged on the floor, causing exquisite shocks of pain to make her moan, as she tried to rub them harder against the rough carpeting. Adam had his thumb buried as far as it would go in her wet depths, while two fingers pressed into her flesh beside her clit. He flexed his hand, and she felt pleasure take over. She could feel the way her body clamped down on his thumb and the finger in her ass, and couldn't have stopped herself from coming if she'd wanted to.

She knew there would be consequences, and flinched as the first smack fell on the cheek of her ass. She didn't see the way her legs flexed to rise for each smack of his hand, but the men did, and they were all smiling when Adam rubbed over the reddened flesh with a firm touch. He reached over into the pile of toys that were in the overstuffed chair, and held up a medium sized training plug, along with a bottle of lube, for the others to see. At the nods of agreement, he lubed up the plug, and his fingers, before snapping the top down on the bottle, before he began to slide the plug into her tightest hole.

Quinn described what Adam was doing in minute detail. She wasn't enjoying this part nearly as much as she'd remembered from the last time. "Do you feel the burn as his fingers open your ass? I remember the way you begged for a hard cock to fuck you in that tight asshole. It took a while to get you comfortable with having a prick so deep inside, that you felt your stomach cramp. The glide of two pricks driving into your slick pussy and ass. You should see what he's doing from this angle, Regina. He just lubed up another finger to stretch you with. Hey, Adam? Why not use the first two fingers of each hand and pull her hole open a bit more? Nothing like what you did to my ass the first few times you half killed me with that monster you call a penis. Eventually, you're going to tap her ass too, she might as well begin as we aim to go on."

Two fingers were enough to make her cry out, so even the thought of a third finger opening her wider, just wasn't something she was excited to entertain right now.

The distraction of the slow, burning ache in her sphincter was doubled as she felt his fingers attempting to pull open that tight muscle. She knew he was going slowly, and appreciated his efforts, but she would just as soon have it done and over with. She knew he was going to plug her as soon as he thought she was ready.

When she felt the tip of the hard, rubber toy enter her ass, she tried to relax her trembling limbs. As it slid easily inside, she concentrated on the small pain of her stretching tunnel. Rather than insert the plug and allow her to come, Adam fucked it into her, as if it was a real prick.

Within minutes of him beginning that stroking motion, she warmed. In fact she was burning up. She needed to be fucked, and she didn't want to wait. He continued to fill her rear. She moaned loudly when he began to use a screwing motion for penetration. She had been reduced to a puddle, lying on the floor crying and begging him to let her come.

He pulled the plug out, leaving her squirming in anticipation, thinking he was going to replace it with his prick. Instead, he urged her to sit up again, steadying her when she swayed as soon as she was upright in his lap again. She wiggled as she felt the thick tip of his cock at her vaginal opening. Gena tried to capture him inside of her slick tunnel, with no luck.

He kept her spread wide, toying with her, before he asked the men watching, "What do you guys think? Has she earned a ride on my prick, or should I leave her like this, and watch her squirm?" She made a strangled noise in her throat as she tried to pull her legs off his, and got a smack on the thigh to stop her.

They must have agreed that she had earned the pleasure of his cock, because she felt him reach down between her legs, taking hold of his prick, and guiding her as she slid down onto his thickness.

He didn't like the angle, and pulled her legs together. He had her stand to face him, before spreading her thighs, and sitting her back down on his lap.

Her thighs were screaming from the stretching, but she wanted that cock more than she wanted to breathe, so she balanced on the balls of her feet and absorbed his prick into her channel. He was thick, and it took her several slides to get him deep enough inside of her for her to sit down.

"Quinn wasn't joking when he described this monster of yours. I'm not sure this is going to work, it feels like I'm being split in two, but I still want it all. Oh, oh, yes. I-" his mouth covered hers, as his hands pushed her hips down over him, making her scream into his open mouth.

She thought that he'd filled her to the brim with the toy in her ass, but this was so much more. She started tightening around his thickness, coming again hard, as his prick started shooting semen deep inside of her. Her muscles were contracting and releasing around him, and he pulled at the nipple clamps, causing her to come even harder. As he unsnapped the clamps from her nipples, she bowed her back, crying out as the blood rushed back into the peaks.

She hadn't passed out, but she wasn't moving either. She hugged Adam as close as she could get, and laid her head on his shoulder. The little moans and shivers bore testament to a very sexually satisfied woman.

They never got around to watching the second video that night. She was worn out, and the men on the computer screen were telling them to get some sleep.

"We should be back by Friday, Sunday at the latest. We can all go out to dinner and talk. And, Regina? Thank you for allowing us to share your pleasure. You are absolutely beautiful." Quinn called her precious, and told her to stay out of trouble.

The computer screen went white, leaving the two of them completely alone. Adam hugged her tight once more, before helping her stand. He steadied her with both hands on her waist until she regained her balance, then he steered her toward the bedroom, for some much needed rest.

Chapter 18

The next morning, she could barely move her legs. The long muscles hurt every time she tried to shift them. Adam ran a tub of very warm water, and carried her into the bathroom so that she could do her business, then crawl into the tub. She groaned when the heat started to work its magic on her muscles. Within a half of an hour, she felt almost human again. Her ass was still sore, reminding her of the pleasures she'd received last night, and her pussy felt like she'd worked those muscles as hard as her legs. She pulled the handle to drain the tub and climbed out.

There was a pot of coffee ready, with a note sitting next to the cup he'd placed nearby.

Had to go home to change and be ready for work today, double shift, will call you later.

It was simply signed Adam.

She was happy that she would have a few hours to herself to think about what she was getting herself into.

Knowing that two of the men were watching, and at times directing her and Adam, gave her a pleasant shiver. She drank her coffee, ate a frozen waffle that she'd browned in the toaster, and started a shopping list for groceries. Not just junk food this time. She would buy meat, potatoes, and healthy things to make salad. Everything one would need to feed a hungry man. She looked at her thighs and sighed. Maybe she would try to begin eating healthier too. Although, with the workout they'd put her through last night, she would be more toned before too many months passed.

She changed the sheets and dusted the condo, before leaving for her shopping trip. She made a detour to the mall, spending two hours window shopping. She finally ended up in front of a women's intimate apparel store. There was a beautiful baby doll nightie, with frothy layers of nylon over satin, in a blueish green color, hanging in the window that she wanted. The nightie was so low cut, that with her boobs, she would be lucky if the cups covered her areolas. It came with a matching thong, and she smiled to herself at the thought of her men seeing her wearing it for their viewing pleasure. She ended up purchasing far more than just the set that had lured her into the store. She left the store with a large bag of lingerie. Each piece had a fantasy involving one or more of the guys attached to it. Just the daydreams alone were incentive enough to buy the items. She smiled all the way to her car. She deposited her purchases in the trunk, then drove to the grocery store.

This was another trip where her purchases were chosen with her men in mind. She'd spent close to two hundred dollars on groceries alone, combining the cost of her earlier purchases of the day, her fantasy men were getting expensive. Though, she couldn't really blame any of it on them. They hadn't asked her to buy any of the stuff.

Back at the condo it took her four trips to haul all of the stuff in, and another hour to put everything away. She still had hours before Adam might call or show up at the door, and she was bored.

There was nothing left to do that needed to be done. Gena clicked on the TV and watched the last half of a John Wayne movie. She laughed out loud when he handed a coal shovel to a younger cowboy so that the young man could spank the girl he was interested in with it. When the movie ended she sat on the couch trying to decide what to do when her cell phone chirped. The number on the caller ID was unknown to her, but she answered the call anyway.

It was Quinn who said hello. She recognized his voice, and she was smiling as soon as she heard him speak.

"We're being delayed by rain. It's coming down so hard, it's like a cow pissing on a rock when it hits the ground, meaning it's really flooding everything, and creating a hell of a mess. Talk to me, precious. How are you today? Tell me what you've been up to."

She cleared her throat, secretly loving that he called her precious, and told him about her boring morning.

"I went to the mall first, where I found some clothes that you may enjoy. After I left there I shopped for food, then I came back here. Nothing very interesting, but it passed the time anyway. I think I will step up my efforts to find a business that I can invest in. I have too many hours and not enough to do, so starting a business will keep me out of everyone's hair, and I won't feel so useless by sitting on my thumbs all day."

He talked her out of making a decision until after they got back and talked.

"We will be playing catch up at home, but before we do anything else, we are coming to see you, and Adam, too. Our main focus will be on you. Do you have any idea how I felt when I heard that some bastard tried to hurt you? I know it's too soon, but I'm not asking for anything other than for you to consider taking us on. We are rude, demanding, over-sexed, and are barely house trained. We watch sports, leave dirty socks on the floor, and fart. But I think you would be woman enough to bring us all back together. Can you do that, Gena? Can you think about building a life with us?"

Since she'd thought of little else but Trey, Quinn, and now Adam, for the past few days, she found herself nodding as she told him, "Yes. I will seriously consider this."

After letting out the breath, he had seemed to be holding, he asked her if she'd watched the other videos. She told him that she hadn't yet. He suggested that it would be a good way for her to pass the time, and that some of the information on the DVD's might help her understand the dynamics of a ménage and poly relationship.

"I'm sure Trey will be calling later today. Right now, he's sleeping. Which is something that I should be doing too, but I wanted to hear your voice."

After they said their goodbyes, she slipped the second video into the machine and sat back to watch. This was an eye opener if ever there was one. The scenes were erotic. Like really erotic. The love showing in the Dom's eyes as he laced his sub's ass and thighs was a surprise, it seemed almost too intimate to watch. As though it should be private. The girl lying spread eagle on the bed, with her wrists and ankles bound to the four posts of the bed, writhed as the whip snapped against her bare flesh.

She called out, begging for more by lifting her ass into the strokes of her Dom's flogger.

Another scene showed a man tying intricate knots in a rope that he was tying his sub up in. The ropes were beautifully manipulated as she smiled as if in a blissful fog.

The next scene shocked as she saw a woman spread over a padded quilt rack, with her ankles tied to either end of the sturdy, wooden piece of furniture. Her ass was red, and any observer could see the handprints decorating her fleshy cheeks. The Dom lubed his fingers, before he used them to invade her asshole. "Holy fuck, that's hot." His fingers weren't taking their time, this was ravishment. Gena felt her own liquid response. By the time he'd begun to stuff inch wide anal beads into her anus, Gena was breathing heavier. When he stuffed her cunt with his cock, while slapping those reddened cheeks, Gena's hand went inside her pants, with two fingers rubbing her clit.

The next scene was of a woman sucking on a thick cock. The man held a clump of hair in his fist as he pistoned his hips, face fucking the willing woman, who was straddling a man lying beneath her. There was another man fingering her small rear hole, and it wasn't long before he replaced his finger with his thick prick. Before the woman on screen came with the three men filling her orifices, Gena was in the lands of a self-manipulated orgasm. It was a good one that lasted for extra seconds. Eventually, she shut the video player off.

The intensity of her orgasm amazed her in the fact that the video had no storylines, only sex acts, and the only words spoken were demands. The women in the scenes, at least the ones she saw, stared at the Dominants as if they worshipped the men. While the looks on the men's faces showed love for their submissive.

There was more to see of the video, but she wanted to think about the way the women acted. Was it all an act? Could a woman actually love three men equally? Could three men love one woman, and not only share her with each other, but remain loyal?

There were really only two ways to find out. She made up her mind, and took a shower, before changing into a short, sassy, emerald green skirt, topped with a satin tailored shirt in a beautiful cinnamon color. Knowing that she was wearing the delicate black lace shelf bra, with matching G-string panties, under the clothing made her feel naughty and feminine. She added black, thigh high stockings, before sliding her feet into four inch fuck me heels, that had tiny bows on the back. She took one last look in the full length mirror before changing her purse to a small clutch. She fluffed her hair, and added a layer of mascara.

It was now or never. She'd been full of enthusiasm and curiosity when she got dressed up like this, now she only hoped that Wesley and Ollie would understand why she planned to ask them to take her to the club where they'd met. She needed answers, and the only way to get them was to see a foursome in action. If she was lucky, there would be a couple of them there tonight. If she was really lucky, she might even get to talk with one of the women in such a situation.

Thankfully, Wesley was home when she knocked on the door. They'd been in the kitchen rinsing dishes to put in the dishwasher. Ollie grinned when Gena explained her reason for the surprise visit, and although Wes looked like he wanted to object to her mission, he finally nodded his head. That was all it took for Ollie to squeal and jump up onto his chest.

"We get to go play at the club, yay."

She pouted when he gave her a swat on her ass.

"You are not playing at the club. We are going as observers tonight, to introduce Gena to one of the foursomes that like to haunt the place on weekdays rather than join the crush on Friday and Saturday nights. She is right to want to research the lifestyle if she is seriously considering a relationship with three men like those guys."

They went to their room to change into something appropriate for the club, and she waited for half an hour for them to get ready. When they did, she had to admire the beautiful couple. Ollie wore a pretty cream colored, loose fitting top, paired with a long clingy skirt of royal blue. Gena had to look twice when she saw her cousin wearing cream colored court shoes with the sexy outfit, but didn't say anything. Wesley looked every bit as yummy as Ollie claimed he did in leather pants, with a black t-shirt under a form fitting, black leather vest that hugged his tight chest. They looked great together, and she told them so.

"No wonder Ollie snapped you up. Damn, Wesley, you look every bit as good as she told me you look in your bad boy clothes." She grinned at the narrow eyed look he gave her. "Now don't get all grumpy on us, you should be happy your wife thinks you are a tasty dish. Be happy I didn't ask you to turn around so I could see that tight ass I've been told about. Not that I'm doubting that you have one, but bouncing quarters off a man's ass means he has to be muscular in that area, you know."

Ollie giggled, and her husband finally grinned, shaking his head at the two women. "Get in the car before I bust that tight little ass of yours, wife. Oh, and, Gena? One more crack like that, and I will make a phone call that will ensure you don't sit with any comfort for a few days. As it is, if Adam finds out you went to the club without him and the others, you could be in for a spanking too, at the very least."

Wednesday nights were habitually slow at the club, and this evening was no exception. Three men had approached them with interested eyes on the two women, but Wes shook his head no, and the men drifted away. As they walked through the communal playroom, Gena stopped dead in her tracks. There were two men kissing. One of the men had his partner's fully erect cock held in a tight grip, as his other hand was working a thin rod into the urethra. She looked to Wes for clarification of what was happening.

"It's a sounding rod, and they come in various sizes, depending on the needs and experience of the users. I tried it once. It can be very pleasurable if you like that kind of play. If they're used on a frequent basis, they will widen the hole. Some men find pleasure to the point of ejaculation while still reaming their cocks out with it. Those that like them are usually masochistic in nature, because it is not a painless practice to start with."

There were six men sitting on the floor, or standing, around a woman that had her hands tied over head, and legs spread wide, while her Dom used a small flogger on her tits. Another man was between her legs licking her clit, while stroking a small dildo into her hairless slit. Wes explained that the three people involved were in a ménage, and the rest were only onlookers.

They went into a hallway where several of the doors were closed, but a few doors were ajar. Wes peeked into each room for mere seconds, until they came to the fourth door. His head came back out, and he looked at Gena,

"This is what you came to see. You will be allowed to watch, but not talk, and no touching. Once they are finished, the men will come into the main rooms, and you can talk to their sub. I know these people, they're a tight group." He pushed her in front of him, the door opening until she was standing close enough to see everything going on in the room. Wes leaned over and whispered, "Remember, be quiet. They know you're here, and have been gracious enough to allow you to see into their private lives. Respect that."

On the way back to Wes and Ollie's, she kept asking them questions about the things that she'd seen. "I couldn't believe how open Freda was about the relationships she shares with her three men. Did you know she has children by all of them? She is like a size six and has six kids. How does she do that? And her men, every one of them, acted like she was the only woman they saw. They obviously adored her. Even the guy that took that skinny whip to her butt, after they'd all come, he put his whole hand inside of her."

The sight of two of the men sucking each other's cocks had almost driven her into an orgasm. When they both came almost simultaneously, she felt her wetness slide down her thighs. That was probably the single hottest thing that she had seen and it stood out in her memory. The grins that both men shared after the fact, showed her that the men enjoyed pleasing each other. It was a dumb thing to pass through her mind, but she was jealous of the confidence the four people showed in their relationship.

Freda had taken all three men, and the hand of the man that Gena secretly considered the mean one. They lubed up fingers and pricks, and all three men had been sucking, or fucking, each other while Freda screamed her release. They'd ended up in a pile of exhausted bodies. She'd shut the door, letting them bask in their afterglow, while she went into the communal rooms to join Wes and Ollie. A short while later, the four came into the room dressed, ready to go home before Wes waylaid them. He took the three men to the bar, after they cleared it with the woman that they clearly adored.

Freda was very open and honest with Gena, even answering the most invasive of questions. Ollie had fallen asleep, so she wasn't chiming in to the conversation. Her most important questions were answered quickly, and with no hesitation. She'd left her with some good advice.

"Honey, there has to be something that intrigued you about them. Something inside of you that told you that they could be trusted, with more than just your body. If you didn't feel safe with them, if you didn't care for them, we wouldn't be here right now. Talk to them. Tell them that you feel like they are trying to railroad you. Don't be too proud to let them in. Listen to them, and make them listen to you. They're men. That means that they don't always think with their big heads first."

"How do you do it? How do you live the lifestyle 24/7?"

"I raise the kids. I do the housework, and it's not like I do it all myself. I have three men who would do anything for me, or our children. I don't mind being at home working to keep up the house, and keep everyone in clean laundry. Plus, do you have any idea how horny three men are? I never go a day without an orgasm, or six..."

The two women exchanged hugs, and Gena woke up Ollie for the ride home.

When they reached the house, Gena hugged Wes, and Ollie, thanking them for helping her better understand what she might be getting into. She got into her car, and drove home, thinking the entire time about everything she had seen, and learned.

The condo was dark when she got home, but the path to her door was well lit, so she wasn't too concerned for her safety. She'd fumbled with her key in the lock, before she was finally able to get it in. She was turning the door handle when a hand clamped over her mouth. She was yanked against the hard body of a man that was still in motion, forcing her to step inside the condo. Her heart was beating so hard that she thought it would explode. Her arms were pulled back, as she felt thin, plastic zip ties cut into her wrists. If she was going to escape, now would be the time. She opened her mouth to scream, and kicked back with one sharp heel, hoping to connect with her assailant's shin. Her heel caught in the material of his pant leg, and when she jerked her leg back for a second shot, they both went down, with him falling heavily on top of her. He was cursing as she felt him stand up. The next thing

she saw were the lights on, and Adam standing over her rubbing his knee.

If she'd thought before she opened her mouth, it would have gone better for her, but she was on an adrenalin rush, and said the first thing that came to mind.

"You son of a bitch," she shrieked. "You scared the hell out of me. When I get loose from these things I am going to kill you. How could you do this to me? Why would you do this to me? I want you to leave."

That little speech got her picked up like a sack of potatoes, and carried into the living room, with her hair brushing the floor. He hadn't said a word the entire time, but when he set her down face first over the back of the couch, she knew he planned to spank her.

She heard him curse as he tried to take her blouse off. She couldn't stop her grin at his fumbling attempts. Her grin dropped when she felt a knife slicing up the back of her favorite blouse. She was pissed that he'd ruined her shirt, and she was pissed that it made her shiver, and not in fear.

"What do you think you're doing? I love this blouse. You have no right to destroy my clothes."

He tossed her skirt over her back, and she knew he wasn't listening to her when she heard him pull his belt from its resting place on his hips.

"I came back early thinking that you might be lonely, that you might want to go for a ride to see something I have been working on. Maybe during the ride you could ask more questions. What I found was that you were not only gone, but that you never thought to turn your outside security light on. It's called a security light for a damn good reason. I have been waiting for you for the past two hours, and what do I see when you get out of the car? I see a vision of a naughty librarian that most teenagers fantasize about, and she never looked right or left to make certain some creep wasn't waiting for her," he growled into her ear. "First this tit jiggling bra, and now a fucking G-string? You went out in public, alone, wearing nothing under a skirt that barely covers the cheeks of your ass, and a fucking G-string?"

The first few slaps of the belt stung, and she squealed. By the time he was done, her ass was on fire, and the tops of her thighs felt raw from his enthusiastic swings of the leather belt.

She was crying, dark brown rivulets running down her cheeks from her mascara. As much as he hated to see her cry, he would bust her ass for such risky behavior every day for a month if it would prevent him being forced to watch her casket being lowered into the ground. He threw the belt across the room, and sliced through the zip ties holding her wrists together behind her back. He rolled her over, and pulled her into a sitting position on the deep cushions, ignoring her gasp as her sore flesh met the nubby cloth.

He left the room, but was back within minutes to lead her into the bathroom where he'd started the shower. He left her some privacy to take care of her needs, and clean up. He went out to his car and got two bags from the trunk. One was his kit, with two clean uniforms and toiletries, the other was a bag from the home improvement store he'd stopped at during his lunch hour.

He locked the door to the condo, and dropped his things on the kitchen table before checking on Gena. He thought she might be crying still, but she was humming a vaguely familiar song. If he remembered it right, the song's lyrics were very suggestive. He rested his head on the door frame. She was fine, it was him that was a fucking wreck.

He'd been worried for two hours as he sat waiting for her to show. When he watched her exit her car showing the tops of her thigh highs, with those heels that made her ass look even more fantastic, he opened his car door to give her a heads up that he was waiting for her. But then she had started walking like it was a sunny day, and he had seen the full outfit. He also saw the way she kept walking without checking her surroundings. Her tits were jiggling, her ass was swaying, and he lost his shit, deciding he needed to teach her a lesson. The problem was, he was the one that learned a lesson.

He wanted Trey and Quinn to get back. Maybe they could help him with his fear of losing her like they'd lost Sara. He couldn't do that again. The pain had been too much. The only thing that kept him from blowing his own brains out, had been the burning need to find the man who shot her and hurt him, hurt him badly. Unfortunately, the leads had been few, and they all led to dead ends.

He told himself he was still around so when they did catch the guy, he would make him pay. Now his focus was changing, and he felt twinges of guilt. Sara would have been the first, and loudest, one to tell them to move on. Would it really be that easy?

Gena came out of the bathroom to see Adam hanging up his uniforms in her closet. It seemed he still didn't want to talk about what was bothering him, so she crawled into bed, pulling the covers over her naked body.

A while later he slid into bed next to her, and pulled her into his arms, hugging her tightly to him.

"Don't ever risk your safety like that again. I lost one woman to violence, I wouldn't survive if I lost you too."

She stayed like that, tucked close to his chest, and knew she was done with the inner struggle concerning if she should or shouldn't go ahead and commit to a relationship with the three men. She was going to allow herself to fall into the lure of their proposition. Being held like this through the night was more comforting than she'd believed possible, and she fell asleep thinking that she was falling in love,

She had coffee brewing, and eggs and sausages frying on the stove, when Adam came into the kitchen the next morning. The sight of her in the short, terrycloth robe made his cock wake up, but he didn't have time for that if he wanted to eat the meal she dished up for him. He hadn't eaten the night before, and was shoveling the food in his mouth like a starving dog when he looked up to see her smiling. He finished the last bite before he picked up his coffee to wash down the delicious meal.

He pulled his wallet from his pocket and extracted a credit card.

"The guys and I decided that since we will be together, we are buying a house and will need furniture. The house has four bedrooms, with three and a half baths, a formal dining room, large family room, living room, and the kitchen has just been updated. I don't have time to shop for everything we will need, but since you can't seem to sit still for five hours at a time, I figure you can do your part. I hate shopping. Any man worth the name knows that women are picky about linens and stuff." He handed the card to her, along with a long kiss. "Pick out what you like. Quinn is color blind, and Trey hates too much orange. A little is fine, but an entire room makes him queasy for some reason. Other than that, whatever you think we need, get it." He wrote an address on an old receipt and handed that to her too.

"Have the furniture delivered tomorrow afternoon to this address. The small stuff we can take over tonight, and you can get the nickel tour. Oh, make sure at least two of the beds are firm mattresses, the other ones are up to you. I'll be off shift around six tonight, so we can catch a meal on our way." He snagged her close for another kiss and left without her ever saying a word.

She sat at the table and stared at the credit card and the address. They were actually committing to living in the area. They were buying a house and wanted her to live there and furnish it. She was cradling her coffee cup, trying to decide where to start on this huge task when her cell phone rang.

"Hello?"

"I forgot to tell you there is no limit on that card, and you are authorized to use it, so don't be shy," Adam said.

The phone went silent in her hand. She picked up the card and saw that it had her name on it. How had he known? Remembering her resolve to do her part to make a new life with three lovers, she cleaned up the breakfast dishes and hurried to get dressed. She had some serious shopping to do, and the knowledge that she was actually furnishing her new home was exciting.

The first stop she made was to a large furniture store. With four bedrooms, the choices had to be made with men's needs in mind. There was a beautiful four poster that got her imagination running. The heavy wooden posts were as thick as small tree trunks, and polished to a shiny honey color. The sales girl zeroed in, explaining the reason for the size of the bed.

"I can't name names, but the guy that ordered that bed plays professional basketball. He ordered both the bed, and the mattress, custom made. A week later he was traded and cancelled the order for the bed. He lost his deposit because he didn't notify us in time to stop production, or delivery to the store. That's why it's so cheap. The linens are a bit pricey, but they are eight hundred thread count, Egyptian cotton. We have three sets with the order."

Gena chose the bed, and a highboy to go with the mirrored dresser. The end tables and lamps were added to the order, along with the sheets and comforter.

By the time she'd bounced on the mattresses of seven other beds, she had only chosen one other bed to be delivered. With no room dimensions, or knowledge of layouts, she was flying blind. She decided to get a comfortable grouping of furnishings for the family room, hoping that it matched the color scheme. It was hard to go wrong when the sofa only had to be a comfortable place to sink your tired body onto after a long day.

Buying linens at the mall also proved to be frustrating. What colors were the bedrooms and bathrooms? She purchased a dozen bath towels in white and dark blue, with matching washcloths and hand towels, thrown into the cart too. By the time she'd walked through the cooking utensils and serving ware, she was a wreck. There was no way she'd be able to furnish the house without actually seeing it first.

She made up her mind, and only bought a four slice toaster, and a coffeemaker. When she got to the grocery store, she knew what to buy. Food didn't depend on room size, or color schemes, and paper plates had no boundaries. They could tough it out for a day or two until she knew what they needed, and could take her time selecting the right things.

She was waiting when Adam got back to the condo. He kissed her hello and took a quick shower before they headed out. On the way to finally seeing the new house, she told him what she'd decided.

"I know you were expecting to have all of the furniture delivered tomorrow, but I couldn't buy a bunch of stuff for a place sight unseen."

They pulled into the driveway of a beautiful, older, two story brick home. The neighboring houses were spaced out so that each property had plenty of room. The landscaping was wooded, so no worries about keeping the grass as short as the neighbors. She stood in the driveway looking at the solid structure, imagining what it would be like to call this place home. "You know something, Adam? I've never lived in an actual house before. My parents rented apartments, and Ollie always had the condo."

He opened the door, and stood back, allowing her to enter the house first. As they toured the rooms, she could see that it was a good thing she'd waited on the major furnishings. While she wrote down notes for each room, Adam brought in the items from her earlier shopping trip, shaking his head at her frugality.

"I told you that you didn't have to worry about money, Gena," he said. That got him a lecture about color schemes and countertops.

Adam suggested that instead of going to a restaurant, they could go back to the condo and order pizza. Now that she had the information she needed to work on her project, she was anxious to get to her computer to check for sales, and general pricing. So she agreed.

Chapter 20

Entering the condo, she sensed that something was different, but when she turned to Adam to say something, she was snatched from behind. She saw his grin before she felt someone bury their face into her shoulder, nuzzling her neck. It was Trey, she just knew it, she remembered the feel of his arms. He turned with her, carrying her into the room where she spotted Quinn grinning at her, as he bent down to give her a scorching kiss.

She ended up on Trey's lap as they ate pizza, and drank sweet tea, while everyone played catch up. The two large pies were gone quickly, with nothing left to prove they'd been there but the greasy cardboard boxes. Quinn told them about relocating the manufacturing plant, and about how they had found out that their partner had been killed by someone's husband when he caught him trying to leave town with the man's wife. "The poor bastard that killed him was turned in by his wife, she thought that since Biscutte had all of that cash for their new life together, she would be able to pocket it and live happy ever after without either man."

Trey got busy disrobing Gena, as Quinn continued the tale. She made a few small noises, but let him have his way. His wide palms cupped her breasts, while his fingers plucked at her nipples.

Quinn stopped talking about their trip, and pulled her off of Trey's lap to stand her up long enough to strip the jeans and panties from her body. Her shoes were tossed aside, and once she was bare, she was bent at the waist, being carried over his shoulder to her bedroom.

"I've been dreaming about the taste of this pussy for the past ten days, so if you have any objections to what I'm about to do, you'd better say so now, because I don't plan to stop until I am damn good and ready." He dropped her on the side of the bed, before he pulled her ass to the edge, pushing her legs wide, and driving his tongue into her wet, pink flesh.

Within seconds she was grabbing the comforter in her fists. When she found a hairy leg next to her, she grabbed onto it, digging her fingers into the muscles. The smooth head of Trey's prick tapped her lips, and she latched on, sucking the meaty muscle into her mouth. When Trey pulled out of her mouth, she whimpered. He gave her a smile, leaning over to kiss her, before pulling her all the way onto the bed, and placing a thick pillow under her shoulder blades. This caused her chest to rise, and her head to fall back. Now she understood why he had moved her. This new angle made it easier for her to take his prick deeper into her mouth and down her throat.

She felt someone else at the mouth of her pussy, and tried to see what the other two men were doing, but all she could see was the shaft of the cock that she was enjoying in her mouth, so she focused on that, working a hand up and down the soft skin. The veins and texture of his cock fascinated her, and she explored the flesh with her fingers, rubbing and tickling. When she felt Trey's cock begin to pulse on her tongue, she tried to suck him in deeper, working her hand around his shaft faster. Her mouth was suddenly flooded with his tangy cum, and she swallowed as much as she could. Her hand continued to work Trey's prick, and she kept sucking as he twitched. He removed her hand from his shaft, and tapped on her jaw to get her to let him go.

"Let it go, Regina. You have me so sensitive that each time you move your tongue the nerve endings feel like electric shocks." She smiled at him for that admission. She had made the big bad Dom cry uncle. There was something very satisfying about that, and if Adam hadn't just entered her in one smooth, but forceful thrust, she might have had time to savor the moment.

Trey pulled the pillow from beneath her, and propped her head on his thigh. His free hand playing with her nipples. He leaned down to whisper into her ear, "Watch this. I never tire of seeing these two together." It was easy for him to say, but she was being skewered on Adam's prick, had Trey pinching her nipples, and was watching as Quinn squirted a large blob of lube onto his fingers.

She knew what he was going to do with that lube, and wished she could watch his fingers penetrate Adam's back hole. The only way she knew that he was actually doing what she thought he was doing, was the way Adam stiffened slightly, changing the angle of his body while still keeping his cock deep inside of her snug tunnel.

*****

"Oh yeah, right there," Adam groaned, and it was music to Quinn's ears. It had been over two years since he'd sunk his cock into the man's asshole, and he had missed it. He'd lubed his cock with more than enough of the slippery stuff to ensure that his lover wasn't going to be in too much pain, a little burn was unavoidable. He knew exactly how Adam was feeling with each inch Quinn claimed as his. The initial stretch and burn, while his thick cock widened the way for the rest of him to slide through the sensitive tunnel of nerves, would only add to Adam's pleasure.

Quinn's prick felt raw each time he pulled slowly out, only to regain the depth he'd claimed. He knew he wasn't going to last, so he reached down, letting his fingers run over the tight sac of Adam's balls, that were currently soaked with juice from Gena's pussy. Knowing Gena was enjoying the extra push he added to the mix, he shoved his hips forward, and as Adam was spurting his cum into Gena, Quinn lost his own battle trying to hold back. He let himself go, coming even harder when he felt the way Adam's channel clamped down on his prick.

His hands ran over the man's back and thighs, soothing him with calming caresses. He curled over Adam's wide back and hugged him. Theirs wasn't a kissy, lovey-dovey relationship. Both men enjoyed having a cock fucking his ass, and they could suck each other off better than any woman ever had.

He would do anything for Adam. There was love between the men, but they usually indulged in trash talk instead of hearts and flowers. The romance was reserved for the woman in their lives. He grinned when he saw that woman lying on her back, still twitching from the orgasms they had given her.

"This bed is too damn small, we need to have at least a California king so we all fit." Trey made his observation while he slid off the bed to go into the bathroom. He came back out with a wet hand towel. He handed the towel to Adam, and told them that they would be sleeping in the other room tonight.

"I am so fucking tired, I could sleep for a week. The only things I would wake up for would be to fuck and eat. Since that's not going to happen, I suggest we all try to rest up for tomorrow. We have an entire storage locker full of things that need to be moved to the new house, and Gena has to get some more furniture so we don't end up on the floor."

Sometime in the early morning, Gena woke up to use the bathroom. She came back to bed, smiling when she saw that Trey had taken her pillow hostage. He was using it to cuddle with in place of her. She wanted to curl up behind him and hold him. After a little back and forth, she gave into the impulse. Her head claimed a small corner of his pillow, but her arms claimed the rest of him. She quickly drifted back to sleep feeling happy with her decision.

By morning, their positions had once again shifted, with her being the cuddled one. As she felt a thick appendage sliding into her from behind, the dynamics of their sleeping position didn't matter in the least. The slow thrust of his strokes into her depths were all that mattered.

He pulled her leg back and over his to open her wider.

"Play with your clit," he growled into her ear, and she was happy to comply. His hand came over her hand to push her fingers further down, where she could feel his cock gliding into her welcoming body. "You can feel what you do to me. Every damn time you are in the vicinity, I get hard, and want to bury my cock in your sweet pink flesh."

He splayed his fingers wide, and his thumb mashed into her clit, while he told her how much he loved being with her like this. "Sometime soon, we are going to pierce your nipples, and the hood of your clit. Knowing how sensitive you are will make me smile when you're not naked with one of us. It's only fair, considering that just the thought of you makes it difficult to walk around. I seem to have a constant hard-on."

Trey pulled out, and she whimpered, as she pushed back, trying to capture his prick to finish what he'd started. When she looked back at him, he was laying on his back, with his head propped on the pillows. She rolled onto all fours, crawling over the top of his body, and used her hand to hold him into position, so she could glide down his shaft. He was smiling as she took him. He was so big, that she had to work herself down his thick cock. Pushing down, only to retreat, and take more on the next slide. So far, she'd never taken all of his length, and wasn't certain she could now, but she was going to try. "I want all of you, every inch." Every time she tried to push deeper, his smooth muscle knocked on her cervix, and she would jerk back.

Those small jabs of pain were addictive. She wanted to feel his body seal to hers, but couldn't get him seated deep enough. "Help me. I want it all, give me all of you." Her fingernails were digging into the thick pads of his chest, and she was trembling in need. Her breathing was erratic, as she held her breath each time she bottomed out.

Trey smiled, later he would torment her by withholding his full length, but right now he needed what she was offering, actually begging for, so he gave it to her. His hands went to her hips, pulling her down as he pushed his hips up, at the same time. She screamed as his cock pushed straight at her cervix, and he kept pushing until she was taking every inch of him. "Hold still for a minute. Try to relax, and you'll find out just how much pleasure you can get with a little pain. If we were trying to get you pregnant, this would be a damn good start. My prick is lined up to shoot semen straight inside your uterus. Chances are you would be pregnant before the end of the night. I can feel your muscles squeezing my cock, but I like it right here, so work those muscles and make both of us come."

His hands left her hips, as he reached up to pinch and roll her nipples between his fingers and thumbs. The harder he squeezed the more her vaginal muscles clamped on his cock. He was getting very close to losing his concentration, so he helped her along by keeping one hand tormenting her nipple, while the other reached behind her hip and stabbed at her smallest entrance. There was more than enough wetness from her body for him to stick his finger inside past the sphincter, and that set her off. The already tight channel tightened even further, with the muscle at the gate of her pussy clamping down almost painfully on his cock.

She could only move a scant inch or so, but he didn't need the friction of movement, the stranglehold her depths had on his cock was more than enough to make him empty his load right where he'd told her he would. The extra slickness of his seed helped him a little, but she was still in the throes of her pleasure, and all he could do was let her ride out the storm.

She was stuck on him. Gena knew that she wouldn't be able to let his prick go from where her body thought it belonged. Those aftershocks dancing through her nerve endings refused to stop, and she twitched with each one.

His big hands stroked her back all the way to her thighs, and up again. Each time she'd had sex and made love with these men, it brought something new to the mix, and that was a wonderful feeling.

She sat up, and watched him flinch from her movement. Remembering his complaint about over stimulating his sensitive prick, made her think about how it must be feeling from the workout they'd just shared.

"Are you alright?" She asked out of concern, but it only got a chuckle from him, and another flinch, as he tried to ease her off his hips. His softening flesh began its long slide out, making her squeak, as it slid over her nerve endings. When it tickled her G-spot, she enjoyed a mini orgasm, while he fought to keep from rolling over with her and immediately withdrawing his over sensitized prick. He took his own advice, letting the feeling roll through him, even as his balls tightened, and he felt the last of the semen leave his sac in answer to the way she continued to clamp and jerk at his prick.

When she suddenly stopped moving and dropped onto his chest, he checked to make certain she was still breathing. He wanted to laugh at the way she'd captured him, holding his cock captive as she rung every bit of pleasure that she could handle out of his body. She was passed out, but her muscles were still gently massaging him. He rolled, withdrawing as quickly as he could. She was still out cold by the time he finished his shower, so he went in search of coffee. Time and use would be his friend when it came to her tight body. Not that he'd ever found any woman that could ride his boy like she just did. He'd had tight pussy before, but never one that refused to allow him to leave until it was finished with him. He was laughing to himself as he walked into the kitchen, and found his two best friends already there.

Quinn was grinning at him, and Adam was watching him with a knowing expression.

"I'm surprised you can walk, man. The first time she did that to me I wondered what kind of God had been watching over me to send a gift like her to mankind. The funny part is, I was damn glad that I have a smaller dick than yours at the time." Adam laughed at the smug look that Trey had on his face. "You boys might have been the first to tap that well, but you should have dug just a few inches deeper to get to the sweetest water."

Quinn wanted to know what they were talking about. "Okay, why don't you comedians explain what you're talking about? Or should I go find Gena and ask her?" That sent both men off again, and he started to rise from his seat. Trey pulled his arm down to the table stopping his movement.

"Our woman has a greedy little pussy, that grabs a man when he is deep inside and refuses to let go of it until she has been completely satisfied. She clamped her muscles down so hard, my prick was in danger of being strangled. It didn't happen until she took all I had to give. As soon as she relaxed enough for my boy to retreat, she clamped down again, my cock was so sensitive I thought I'd be coming blood. After a while her vag will get used to taking a thick prick deep, until then, we need to be cautious if we want our cocks to be in working order when she's finished with them." He grinned as he shifted in the hard seat of the chair. "Our girl has skills."

Quinn was staring at Trey, had he actually admitted that a woman got the better of him? "Are you fucking kidding me here? The badass, sadistic Dom got caught in a pussy trap? I swear I gotta see this." He got a glare, and a grin, as his friend nodded his head.

"You think I'm joking? You go right ahead and give her all you have, buddy. Just ask your partner over there, see him grinning?" Adam was actually laughing and nodding his head.

Speaking between snorts of laughter, Adam clasped Quinn's shoulder. "You know how I say you got the tightest ass? Well her pussy is the tightest thing my prick has ever been in when she clamped those muscles down on me. I swear, I was afraid poor old Melvin was gonna be pinched off. Trouble is, I couldn't have cared less at the time, and you know how much I like Melvin."

His solemn last words had them all grinning. Adam insisted on calling his cock Melvin. He'd told them once that his mother heard him making noises while masturbating once and she asked him if he was all right, he'd made up an invisible friend so she stopped asking. She hadn't wanted to encourage her only child by buying into something so silly.

Chapter 21

For the next two days Gena shopped. She forced the men into going appliance shopping, and once they were done, the guys vowed never to step foot in another appliance store with her again. Rather than choosing a machine, she kept asking questions and wasting time making the salespeople find the answers if they didn't have them off the top of their heads.

Quinn complained bitterly when his companions snuck away to the electronics department, leaving him alone with her, while she debated the merits of washers and dryers. Finally, he'd gotten so tired of standing there listening to her, that he'd pointed to the most expensive set, told the salesman to put it on the damned truck, and deliver it Monday.

He pulled her to the back of the store, where the TVs and stereo systems were kept, and found Trey and Adam playing a video game, while the clerk was setting up delivery for the LED flat screens.

"You two owe me, you chicken shit fuckers. She had me ready to run screaming out the door, but then I remembered that you have the keys to the damn car. If I hear another word about load capacity or electronic settings, I am going to do some serious damage to someone's ass." He glared at Gena when he spoke the last sentence, and the clerk looked up at that moment as if he wanted to ask if everything was all right. He took one look at Quinn and ducked his head again.

They got back to the car, and the men had to rearrange the bags and boxes in the trunk and backseat so they would all fit. Gena was getting fed up with their bitching and complaints. It wasn't her fault Mother Nature had put a stop to more than a blowjob for each of them this morning. The only satisfaction she'd gotten was knowing that she had made her men tremble and lose control with her mouth and hands.

For some reason, the fact that she hadn't orgasmed during playtime pissed all three men off, and the day had only deteriorated from there. Well, that was too damn bad, she had cramps, and she was flowing like a stuck hog, she didn't need their attitude. As soon as they got to the house she demanded to be taken to the condo.

"I've had it with the way you guys are acting. I'm a woman, get over it. I'm breaking my neck here trying to get everything for this house, that I might or might not be living in, because no one has asked or invited me to join you here." She wagged her finger at them ticking off her reasons to be mad at them, instead of taking their crap. "I have a college degree in Business, with a minor in Economics. I ask questions to make certain I get the best items for the dollars spent. Rather than thank me, you whine like little boys. I did everything I could to make you happy this morning, and instead of being happy to get a blow job, you act like I'd put salt in your coffee. I've had it. Enough. Do you hear me? One of you take me home. All I want to do is take a hot bath and crawl into bed with my heating pad. Now, will you please take me home, or do I have to call a cab, because I'm leaving one way or the other." She went to the front door and walked outside. Trey came out almost immediately after she'd shut the door, and led the way to his vehicle.

When they arrived at the condo, he walked her to the door, and came inside with her. She ignored him, as she put a cup of water in the microwave to heat up for tea. She didn't offer him anything, but he sat down on one of the kitchen chairs anyway, before he snagged her arm and pulled her onto his lap. She half-heartedly tried to resist, but he held her firm to his chest.

"I'm sorry that you aren't feeling well, you never said a word about having cramps or that your back ached. You need to learn to tell us this stuff, we can't read your mind any better than you can read ours. The reason I was in a pissy mood this morning is that I get as much, or more, satisfaction from seeing you enjoy sex as much as I'm enjoying it, preferably at the same time. When you just smiled and kissed me after the fantastic way you sucked my cock, I could tell that you hadn't gotten much, if anything, out of it. My ego got dumped on. I'm not used to one-sided pleasure, unless I'm the one giving it." His big hand massaged her lower back, and she relaxed more. "I can't speak for the others, but I believe they feel like I did this morning.

"You should also know that you're the reason that we bought that home. Without you there, it's just a house. I see the care and love that you're pouring into it, and I do appreciate the hard work. We all do. But you need to cut us a little slack too. When you are hurting, or don't feel well, say something. We're men, not mind readers. We scratch our asses, belch, fart, and will do our best to stay out of the way when we've done something we are not very proud of. Like taking our pleasure this morning without returning the favor.

"Quinn and I will be going to Wisconsin the day after tomorrow. We need to close up the offices there, and take care of the business of moving the offices back to Michigan. It's not a big deal because we have a very small staff, but we need to take care of a few things. We'll be back by the end of the week. Adam is resigning from the police department, and is going to take up his law practice again. We need a lawyer to handle the day-to-day contracts, as well as, matters like this last partnership that went sour. When we get back, all of us are going to have a major discussion about our futures."

He didn't leave until she'd had a shower since she'd decided the bath was too much trouble. He put a mug of tea on the nightstand, and made sure the heating pad was working correctly. He left the room, and came back with a few, individually wrapped, chocolate candy bars that he'd found in the cupboard. He set them next to the mug and leaned over for a tender kiss. "Sleep, sweetheart. We'll check in on you later. Don't worry about dinner, we'll take care of it."

He was being so nice that she wanted to have him come back and hold her, but she had to establish some lines of respect.

"Thank you for the way you've been since we got here, but you need to understand my side of things. I'm not your Sara. I'm me, Regina. If all I am is a substitute for your lost love, please don't come back here. I want a future with a man, or men, that love me because I'm worth loving, not because they want to recapture what they've had in the past. I have a brain, and I have common sense. I don't mind being submissive during sex, in fact, I like it. But I'll be damned if I stand by while you guys take your petty bullshit complaints out on me." She laid back on the pillows, and gave him a tired smile, "Don't expect blowjobs every morning either, especially when I have days like this."

*****

Trey locked up as he left, and headed back to the house. She was right on a number of points, and one item she'd touched on was like an elephant, in a tutu, sitting at a bar. No one wanted to mention that it was there, even if they could plainly see the thing.

Adam and Quinn were setting up the basement playroom, and the weight room. They'd made plenty of headway reassembling the weight machines and racks, and he was happy to see that he would be able to pump some iron to relieve the tension in his shoulders tonight. Right now, they had somewhere to go.

"Come on guys, we're going on a short road trip," he told them. His closed expression was met with raised eyebrows, but they followed him up the stairs and out of the house, piling into the car without a word. They both wanted to know where they were going, but all he would tell them was, "Somewhere we should have gone the day we decided to keep Gena as ours."

When he pulled the car through the gates, and onto the winding path, there was no doubt in anyone's mind what he'd meant. They left the vehicle, and walked perhaps a hundred feet, until they stood over the single headstone where Sara's body rested. They'd picked a beautiful, pink granite headstone and her name was written in thin block letters. It had been over two years since she'd passed, and the small shrubs that they'd planted six months after they had laid her to rest, were now small conical trees.

Adam confessed to paying the groundskeepers to keep the bushes trimmed neatly. "I come here about once a year, just to sit talking to myself. She's not here, guys. She left us, and her soul is in heaven with our baby." He sat on the thick grass and hung his head. "I knew she was pregnant, but I was waiting for her to tell us. She was puking her guts up, and I saw the box the pregnancy test came in when I took out the trash. If I'd let on I knew, maybe she wouldn't have felt she needed to buy that Champaign.

"Her mother died last year. Did you know that? She's buried over in the old section of the cemetery with Sara's dad. I was thinking about having her moved so she wouldn't be so alone here." He looked up as the two men joined him on the grass. "I procrastinated because there were days that I would look at my gun and think about how easy it would be to stop the pain. To no longer feel like my heart was being ripped out of my chest one strand of muscle at a time. And one night, a year to the day she was murdered, I put everything in order. I wrote out my will, threw out the perishables that were in the fridge, and even called into work to tell them I was sick and might not be in for a few days. I dressed in the suit I wore to her funeral, and decided to end the pain in the bed we'd all shared.

"I remember that I was checking the chamber to make sure it was loaded, for probably the tenth time, and felt her hand on my head. I know it sounds fucked up, but she came to me. She told me not to do it. She told me that she was all right, and that the baby was playing with the angels. Sara told me that the angels were spoiling our baby. She said that I had someone else who would need me, and that you guys needed me too." He wiped his hand down his face, and shook his head before continuing, "I don't remember how, or what happened, but I woke up the next day on the bed. My gun was on the nightstand, and it was almost noon."

Quinn nodded his head because he believed every word Adam had said. "I tried to drown my sorrows in booze. One night I wrapped the Harley around a tree, and somehow landed in the freezing waters of a lake. I walked away without a scratch on me, and by the time the cops got there, I was as sober as could be. I felt someone toss me into that lake. I didn't want to tell anybody about it because I was ashamed of myself. I still believe it was Sara who saved me from the same fate as my Harley."

Trey looked away from the cold granite stone and studied the grass under his fingertips. Glancing up, he met Quinn's eyes and shrugged his wide shoulders. "How do you think I happened to be on that road at three in the morning? I'd been working, and must have fallen asleep at my desk. The next thing I knew, someone slapped the back of my head and told me to wake up. While I was trying to see who was in the room with me, I heard a voice telling me to go to where you were. I believe the words were something like, '*You're the lead man here, and failing miserably at it. Been There and Done That are lost, and all you can do is sit here and wallow. Quinn needs you*.' I got in the truck and started driving. I didn't even lock the house when I left. All the way there I kept hearing the words 'fix this,' and when she wasn't haunting me with that, she said 'find her." He shook his head, and took a deep breath. "That's why I started going back to the old haunts. It wasn't because I couldn't wait another day to nail some pretty little sub. The night I first laid eyes on Gena, I swear I could hear clapping, and the words 'Yes, that's her.'

"I could see that Quinn was as attracted to her as I was, so when we got the call about the plant overseas, I called you, Adam."

Trey looked at his best friends, and got down to business. "Gena thinks she is a substitute for Sara. In fact, she made a point of telling me tonight that she wasn't Sara. She's a person in her own right, and our girl made it clear that she's not going to put up with our old baggage. So let's deal with what has been haunting us, because I'm not giving up on my future happiness. We were blessed to have Sara in our lives, but she's gone, and she might not have smacked you two on the head, but she damn sure did me. Between the

smack, and then the punch to the heart Gena gave me today, I'm ready to move on."

Quinn closed his eyes, and let his own pain flow through his body. When Trey mentioned Sara's pet name for him and Adam, it choked him up. She'd called them Been There and Done That, because where ever they'd gone and whatever they'd done, it had usually been done together.

"You know it occurs to me that we've spent very little time actually getting to know Gena. I don't know her favorite color, or if she likes dogs or cats. I have no idea if she likes kids, or even when her birthday is. I can tell you where every freckle is located on her body, and where to touch her to make her shiver. The taste of her is stamped into my brain, but I'll be damned if I know much of anything about her life. What kind of man does that make me? She's right, I need to know her." Quinn got up and walked back to the car.

Adam was dealing with his own thoughts, and remembered something. "Sara told me that night that another woman needed me. I couldn't save Sara from the guy who killed her, but I did save Gena from that creep. I should tell Quinn that her favorite color is green, and her birthday is on Halloween." He followed Quinn, leaving Trey alone to talk to Sara.

"You know, I loved you, and so did the others. Thank you for every day you gave me and the guys. I want to thank you for the future too. I- we, have a future to start working on.

Her name is Gena, and she's waiting for us."
He kissed his fingertips, before laying them on
top of the stone. He didn't look back as he went
to join his partners.

Chapter 22

She had put the last throw pillow on the couch, and the last clean dish in the cupboard. Now it was time to go back to the condo and have a nice hot soak in the tub, maybe she'd even paint her toenails. The guys would be back tomorrow, and she wanted to look as good as she could when she saw them again.

The last time she'd laid eyes on one of them had been the night of her meltdown. Quinn had brought dinner for the two of them, and over a delicious meal of takeout chicken and potato salad, they'd talked. He'd asked her question after question about her life and what she liked to do. She couldn't believe how much information he'd pried out of her that night. Now he knew almost everything about her. She had told him about her parents' deaths, and her, not so shining, moment when her prom date, Travis Henry, took her virginity in the backseat of his mother's minivan. Both of those events had been epic in their own ways. She'd lost her parents, but gained Ollie. With Travis, she'd gone to prom with a hunky football player, and ended up losing any admiration for him in the end. He was a selfish little boy in a masculine body. The last time she had heard anyone talking about him, they said he was living with his parents, and working at a sporting goods store.

Most of her personal things were ready to pack. Where each man had talked to her about living in the house, none of them had ever actually asked her to live with them. She didn't want to assume that they would. No future plans had been discussed, nor had anyone asked for her opinion. Until they asked, she was staying right here.

She didn't need them to survive, there was no desperation in her housing, financial needs, or job search. If she went to live with the men, she would go because they gave her a damn good reason to be with them. That reason had to be love. She was worthy of love, and had resolved not to cave in on the issue. If they couldn't come to her whole hearted, they could enjoy continuing to wallow in their misery. She wasn't going to beg for leftovers.

At the condo, she poured herself a glass of wine, drinking it while she enjoyed a hot bath scented with cinnamon oil and vitamin E. It was a mixture that she had discovered while she was in college, trying to get through chemistry class without failing. The cinnamon smelled divine, and the vitamin E gave her skin a silky feeling. Combined with the relaxing effects of the hot water and wine, she was feeling relaxed and happy.

After her bath, she grinned when she saw her reflection in the mirror. She'd donned the new baby doll nightie, feeling sexy and confident in her appearance. Her reflection no longer making her cringe. If fact, she looked hot. "If they could see me now, they would be on their knees." She giggled as she poured another glass of wine, and got her manicure set from the dresser.

Choosing which color to paint her toenails wasn't as easy as it should have been, but she settled on a shiny black cherry. She was finishing the pinky toe on her right foot when her cell phone began to chirp. Checking the caller id, she smiled. It was Trey, and if this call was the usual late night type of call they shared, her feelings of looking sexy were a good thing. He liked to call her and tell some of the things he planned to do with her when he was back in town.

"You sound like you're in a good mood. Are you ready for me to fulfill all of the promises I've been making to you?"

The sound of his voice made her nipples go hard. "What promises would those be? The one where you plan to make mad, passionate love to me? Carry me away on your pirate ship? Or the one where you…" She couldn't keep it up. The giggles took hold and it took several minutes before she sobered.

"Adam should be there by now. He's picking you up, and bringing you home. We got home early and have missed you. It's chilly out, so wear a jacket."

The line went dead, and she hurried to find a coat. Thinking about their faces when she took the coat off was exciting. She stuck her feet in a pair of ballet flats, and waited by the door with her purse. Within seconds the doorbell chimed, and she looked to make sure it was Adam. It was him all right, handsome as ever, and looking sexy in a leather jacket, standing on the other side of her door. She opened the door, and locked it, before stepping outside.

"Hi, Trey just called and told me to grab my coat, so I was ready for you to pick me up."

He pulled her close for a deep kiss that left them both breathing heavier, before taking her hand, and leading her to the Road Runner. In less than fifteen minutes, they pulled into the garage at the house. He hadn't said much since saying he'd missed her and was happy to be back.

They walked into the kitchen and she barely had time to say hi, before being snagged by Quinn and kissed breathless. He didn't even set her down, he just handed her off to Trey, who basically fucked her mouth. He steadied her before stepping back. The words, "We need to talk," were not entirely unexpected since Adam reminded them.

Trey led her to one of the dining room chairs, and sat her on it. He offered to take her coat and she declined to remove it. The men stood in front of her and offered an enticement.

Trey's was, "Come and join us in the playroom, I want to show you my collection of whips and cuffs."

Quinn's contribution was, ''Join us in the playroom and I'll let you watch me fuck Adam.

If you're quick to get down there, I might be nice enough to let you lube his ass, and prime my cock." Damn him and his smile. She'd told him how hot it was when she watched the two of them having sex with each other, so now he was using the information as a lure.

Adam smiled at her and wiggled his eyebrows, before offering his arm for her to take. "Feeling brave?" She took the offered arm, and was led to the door separating the playroom from the weight room. Outside of the door was a small table that displayed a single item on top. It was the leather collar that Adam had put on her back in the early days when she had just started to learn how to please him.

"I'm going to join Trey and Quinn inside. If you decide to join us, drop the coat, and put the collar on, before you enter this room. Keep this in mind, sweetheart, if you come through that door collared, and drop to your knees once you are inside, you are ours. For keeps." He kissed her forehead, and went inside the room, leaving her to make the decision without further persuasion.

Theirs. She would be theirs, for keeps. If this was their idea of romance, then she was going to have to teach them what romance actually consisted of. She dropped the coat next to the table, and picked up the collar. It was time to claim her men.

They waited for her to open the door. Each man hoping that she would decide to stay. The past few days had been devoted to removing any remnants of past regrets and emotional burdens. Their love for Sara would always be in their hearts, but their future was on the other side of the door.

What seemed like hours, was actually only minutes before the door finally opened, and their nightie-wearing sub came into the room. Her hair was pulled up in a messy ponytail, and the collar was buckled in place where it belonged on her neck.

She went to her knees and bowed her head, waiting for someone to speak. Her panties were in the pocket of her coat. She knew they wouldn't be needed, and when Trey took her hand to help her stand, she knew it was the right decision. The pretty slip of satin was whisked over her head and tossed into the corner.

The smiles that she saw on their faces was worth the worry of the past days.

*****

"You wanted the real men, well, tonight you are going to get what you asked for. It's too late to change your mind, sweetheart. By the time this night is over, you will know each of us in every way possible." Trey took her over to the two men who were kissing. "They are so masculine that it makes you want to fuck them, right?" Trey reached around her to pick up a plastic bottle of lube. He opened it, then held her hand palm up. "Here you go. Let's give them a little help, shall we? You go behind Adam and make sure his asshole is nice and slick. His prick is longer than Quinn's, but Quinn's is thicker, so you need to use at least three fingers to stretch him. Can you do that for them?"

He poured a generous amount of the gel onto her fingers, and led her hand to the crack of Adam's split. Her first finger, and his, slid through the tight spot until they touched the small hole. "Adam, spread your legs so our girl can join in the fun here. She's already creaming, just watching you two." As soon as Adam spread his legs a bit, Trey pushed her slick finger inside the tight opening. She wiggled her finger a little, exploring the texture of his inner muscle. It was smooth, and very elastic.

She didn't need assistance to add a second finger. She twisted her hand a half turn and back, pushed two fingers to the second knuckle, and then tried to open her fingers in a scissoring motion, but didn't have the strength to keep them apart for more than a few seconds. "I think I need more lube, I'm afraid I'll hurt him. I can't believe how tight this is." Trey poured more gel into the crack of Adam's ass so she wouldn't have to pull her fingers out. The additional lube made adding another finger much easier, and soon she was doing her best to finger fuck his hole, while she kissed and licked her way over his back. Feeling him shiver, as she licked her way down his spine, made her feel powerful. This man, this tough guy who drove a muscle car and carried a gun, shivered as she fucked his ass with her fingers. Trey slid his hand up and under hers, adding one of his thick digits to the steady rhythm of her own. She grinned when Adam stiffened and bent at the waist to take Quinn's cock in his hands. She did some shivering of her own, when he began licking the large, dark pink head.

Trey took his fingers away, leaving her busily reaming Adam's hole while she listened to his moans. She used her other hand to lightly scratch the underside of his nutsack. That brought more shivers, and another groan from him.

She squeaked when her hand was removed from Adam's flesh. Trey wiped her hand with a wet wipe, before she was taken to the padded trunk a few feet away.

"It's your turn, darling. I owe you a good spanking, but first things first. Reach inside the trunk and pick an anal plug." She lifted the lid, looking at the collection of colorful anal plugs. She finally picked one that looked to be about the size of the ones she had back at the condo. When she held it out to him, he shook his head.

"No, you need a larger one for tonight. Before tonight is over, you will have all three of your holes filled and fucked, at least once. I want you as wide and open as you can get. Remember? We want your enjoyment too." He leaned down and kissed her, before trailing his lips to her jaw and up to her earlobe. He took the small fleshy skin in between his teeth, biting down until she moaned. "I want to hear you scream when I slide my cock into your ass, and know that you are loving the burn and bite of pain while I fuck you senseless. Reach into the trunk, and grab the purple one. We will save the big one for later. I can't wait to hear you cry for relief while I torment you just a little."

She reached back down, and picked up the requested toy. It was thicker than the last one she had chosen. Her nerves almost got the best of her. It wasn't like she hadn't had his cock in her ass before, but for some reason, the toy seemed daunting.

"We good here?" He asked. She answered with a nod. He grinned as he helped her lie over an odd looking bench seat. He fastened her feet to the legs of the contraption, and she squeaked when the padded spot tilted forward, taking her with it so she was almost folded in half, while standing on her tip toes. She wanted to know what was coming, but he was talking to Quinn and Adam. The position she was in allowed her to turn her head, but that was about it.

"Uh, excuse me, this is not the most comfortable position I have been in so far. If you could stand me up it would probably take care of the problem." From the look she received from Trey, you'd think she'd asked to trade places. He moved from her sight and the next thing she felt was a rubber ball being pushed between her lips, that had just gasped from the stinging swat she'd she felt on her thigh. He fastened the thing behind her head. This was out of her wheelhouse of expertise, but hindsight told her that she wasn't supposed to talk in a submissive role, unless she was asked a direct question.

The position was still uncomfortable, and she wanted to watch Adam take Quinn's prick into his body. The idea, and images, that that wish brought to her mind made her even wetter. She could feel her juices sliding down her thighs at this point.

The slap of Trey's hand on her ass brought her focus back to her predicament. The continued swats increased in intensity, then stopped altogether. She tried to tell him to fuck her, but with the ball in her mouth, plus his fingers playing in the wetness coating her labia and vulva, all she could do was moan.

"It looks like you need this now. I can see the way your greedy little hole is clenching each time I smack this beautiful ass. Here you go now, sweety. We'll get this good and deep. If you're nice and cream for me, I might let you suck Adam's cock while Quinn reams his ass. Judging how your snatch just gripped my fingers, I guess you like that idea. By the way, if you need us to stop at anytime, take this." He placed a metal ball in her hand with a chain that fastened to her wrist. The chain was long enough to hit the floor if she dropped it, but the small band held it to the first knuckle of her finger so her hands could open and close at will. All she had to do was flick it off her finger and it would hit the floor.

He'd obviously lubed his fingers well as she felt them slide into her rear hole with very little discomfort. The deeper those fingers went, the wider they stretched her, causing that burn she remembered from the last time. She also remembered the deeper he went, the more she liked it. If he would just get with the program, she would have another mind-blowing orgasm.

She felt his fingers leave her body, and whimpered at the loss. The introduction of the purple plug was larger than his fingers had been. As it slid through the tight muscled ring, stretching it to the point of painful burning, she screamed. This was like having Quinn's cock working its way into her smallest opening. His hand continued to steadily push the toy, as his other hand rubbed over the small of her back. No matter how many moans or whimpers she made, he was unrelenting in his purpose to seat the thing as deep as it would go.

"Two more inches. Just two more inches, Regina. Are you enjoying the burn? I know it's larger than what you're used to, but this hole will be a favorite of ours once you learn to take our pricks inside. We have to be careful not to damage you. So, slowly at first, then I'm going to give it to you as fast and deep as you want it. Look at this beautiful pussy crying for a cock. Damn, sweet, you are soaked." He pushed the plug in deeper and she screamed in pain for real, until he began sliding it in and back out a few inches at a time.

Her clenching hole gripped onto the toy, and the harder she gripped it, the deeper she began to breathe. When he slid it inside, seating it fully, she gave up all attempts to stop the orgasm that shook her body. The gag was removed, and she verbalized her ecstasy with a short scream. "Fuck, that burns, and hurts, but if you take it out I'll kill you..."

She heard laughter, and looked sideways at Quinn and Adam. They were seated on the floor watching Trey work on her ass, as they stroked each other's pricks. She tried to straighten her body to a standing position, but Trey had to tilt the bench up to allow her to stand. He untied her ankles, and pushed her in the direction of the two men on the floor.

It wasn't easy to walk the six steps she had to take to reach the men. Quinn reached for her hand to bring her down to the floor, and she couldn't stifle the yelp when her butt connected with the floor. It drove the plug deeper, and she was already so sensitive that if one of the men touched her soaked clit, she would go off again.

Quinn and Adam laid her onto her back and spread her thighs, before they took turns licking the juices from her thighs and slit.

"Awe, sweet precious, you know how much I love the taste of your pussy. Come on, give me more. I have to share with Adam, but that's alright, isn't it? He's going to let you suck his cock while I fuck his tight ass, so we will be enjoying each other all together. Hmmm, I bet if you ask Trey nicely, he might even take the toy out of your ass and fuck you. Would you like that? Come on, it's time to get Adam ready again. You get to prep his ass for me. You liked that, didn't you?" He sat up from between her legs, easily catching the lube Trey tossed to him. Then he took her fingers, coating them generously.

She turned to Adam, who leaned down and kissed her with long strokes of his tongue along hers. He pulled her arms behind his hips, urging her hand between his cheeks. She started with one finger, then quickly added the next. Each time she pulled her fingers back, his tongue would retreat from her mouth to rest just inside of her lips.

"Fuck, precious, you do that so well I could come from just watching you. Hold his cheeks open for me," Quinn instructed.

She pulled her fingers back, and grabbed Adam's cheeks, but he took her hands away for the few seconds it took for him to lay her head down on the floor, while he crouched over her. Her face now in line with his prick. She reached between his thighs, holding his cheeks apart, while she watched Quinn's thick cock begin its journey into Adam's hole. The sight was crazy exciting to see.

"Oh my, this is indescribable. So damn sexy. I can't believe how big of a turn on it is to watch you two." She let her fingers sneak up between Quinn's thighs, and stroked his sac. "How beautiful, no wonder you guys like porn so much."

Once Quinn was seated deep, there was nothing for her to see, until he began to piston into Adam's body, so she grabbed the thick cock that was bobbing and sliding over her cheek, and pulled it gently to her mouth to lick. The angle made it hard for her to take him into her mouth, so she kissed and licked everywhere she could reach. The touch on her ankle reminded her that Trey was still there, and she wondered what he planned to do.

It was her turn to gasp again, as he began to pull steadily on the plug's flanged knob. He planted her feet flat on the floor, spread as wide as possible, before he began to lightly tease her with his fingers. As the plug came out, she enjoyed the feel of every inch of it. Moments later, she felt the head of his cock sliding through the slick tunnel of her pussy.

"Here you go, go ahead and take what you want this first time. The next round you should be relaxed and limber enough to take any of us in any hole."

By the time she was completely out of her mind ready to come, her knees hung over Trey's forearms. At the first hard grip of her hands on Adam's cock, he pulled them away, placing her hands on the backs of his thighs to hold onto. His big hands were squeezing her breasts, while his thumbs tormented her nipples.

She glanced up to see Quinn's prick sliding between the cheeks of Adam's ass. She loved that she could feel his thighs tremble as he grunted and groaned. Trey was deep inside of her body, and when he began to rub her clit, she shattered.

"I'm coming. Oh, God, yes. I'm coming."

Her screamed announcement set off the men's orgasms, as first she felt her breasts being showered in Adam's semen, while Quinn shouted his release behind him. Trey surged deeper, continuing to mash her clit, while her inner muscles squeezed the cum from his cock. The shouting and groans made her enjoy the moment even more.

She giggled. It was the only thing she could do right now to express her happiness.

She was the one that had caused these big, strong men to collapse. They were all breathless, and wrung out. Not to mention, she was still twitching with the aftershocks from her own orgasm.

What else could a woman ask for?

Adam and Quinn untangled and groaned as they stood. Trey drew his cock from her body, feeling the familiar clamp down on his prick as it slid over her G-spot. She gasped as her hands pulled his shoulders closer to her body while she rode out her second orgasm on his softening cock.

"Stick a fork in me guys, I'm done," Gena groaned, getting a laugh from Quinn.

Quinn helped her rise to her feet, then picked her up and carried her into the next room that had a big tiled shower.

While he soaped her body, taking special care to make certain all of her spots were washed and rinsed clean, Quinn said, "Precious, as long as there is breath in my body, you will never be done. It was hot, knowing that you were watching me fuck Adam. Maybe we'll get you a strap-on so you can join in the ass play sometime. Just about any man likes a finger stuck in his ass when he's fucking, I happen to like something bigger than a finger." They left the shower, and went upstairs to join the others. Gena was only wearing a towel, until Quinn fetched one of his long sleeved button down shirts. She came out of the bedroom with the shirt folded over at the neck, buttoned up, and the arms were tied together under her breasts, with the cuffs tucked into the tight band of the sleeves. It made a short dress on her, but every man was impressed.

Trey sat her on the dining room table, while the men arranged their chairs in a short semi-circle in front of her. She knew this was it. They were going to ask her to move in with them and she could hardly wait. There was no way she would ruin this moment by saying yes before they asked. She deserved this part of the relationship, and she felt she actually needed the words.

"Regina, I have come to care about you more than I ever believed possible. I'm asking you to live with us, and be our woman. You can pick one of us to marry for legal purposes, knowing that when you marry one, you are really marrying all of us." Trey said, then he leaned forward to brush his lips on hers. "I love you, will you be ours?" He produced a plain, white gold wedding band, and held his hand out for her to place her hand into his. At her "yes," he smiled and slid it over her ring finger.

Adam was already on his feet, waiting for his turn. He'd been married to Sara, and Gena wondered if his feelings were deeper for the woman than those of the other men. Gena waited to hear him out, if she detected the slightest hesitancy in what he had to say, it would break her heart, but there was nothing that she could do, or say, that could stop the pain of the loss of a spouse. Grieving took time, and she needed him whole, with no regrets, or feelings of guilt for loving her.

"I need to explain something to you, before I tell you how I feel about you." He took her hand in his, looking directly into her eyes while speaking, "I loved Sara. We all did. Before meeting you, all I had was a thirst for revenge to keep me from eating a bullet and joining her. I tried to shut down all of my emotions. Hell, you've seen the mess I've made of that already, and you even have the book I wrote about my grief and guilt. It took the sight of you to rattle me out of my grief.

"At first, you were a favor to my friends, but that stopped before it even started. Your courage and enthusiasm for life gave me the courage to face myself in the mirror, to come to terms with what I'd become. The day I tackled that sick motherfucker in front of you, it busted down the last wall I'd built. I couldn't save Sara, but I saved you. Even if we weren't together again after that, you changed me. It was sexual, I won't deny that, but it soon became apparent to me that it was so much more than just sex." He cleared his throat, looking away from her, before he looked back.

He took a deep breath, "I love you. Not because I miss having a wife, and not because of the two clowns here. I love you for no other reason than you are my woman, in here," he placed her hand over his heart. "Will you give me the chance for a second life? Will you love me, and let me love you, for the rest of my time on earth?" He wiped the tears that trailed down her cheeks, and took her hand again. He placed a bright gold ring over the top of the one Trey had already placed on her finger. She hugged him to her for a few minutes, until Quinn pushed him out of the way playfully.

"Enough mushy, squishy stuff. This is how it is, precious. I wanted you from the minute I saw you sitting in that restaurant. I'm being truthful, when I tell you that I love you, but I'm more of a show and prove type of guy, so if there is anything you need from me, or any of us for that matter, to prove that we love you and will cherish you until the end of time, all you have to do is ask." She shook her head, smiling through watery eyes.

"I love you all too, but will I always be enough for you?"

After hoots and laughter, Quinn sobered to say, "Precious, you are enough to keep six men happy. Now, about that spanking I owe you, let's test that theory shall we?" The others watched with smiles as he slipped his platinum band over theirs. With encouragement from Trey and Adam, he tossed her over his shoulder, and headed for the playroom.

Gena pouted at Quinn as he slowly swung the leather paddle. She was as trussed up as a Christmas goose, with her wrists locked together overhead and a metal spreader bar holding her ankles apart. She couldn't imagine that her life would ever be boring. The future looked pretty good from every angle she could see. Her next words made the men nod and grin.

"I love you, guys. We're all lucky enough to have our Happy Ever After."

Lynn Ray Lewis

*I love writing Erotic Fiction.
Give me peace and quiet or a set of
headphones and a good music library and I will
write until my hands hurt. Then I will lay in bed
and think of what my characters will do or say
next.*

By Lynn Ray Lewis

Jody's Men
Regina's Men
Mackie's Men
Lucy's Men

A Place For Her (Hade's Temple Book 1)

I Waited For You (Gaurdians Book 1)

Rane's Giants (Tremble Island Book 1)
Hawk's Nest (Tremble Island Book 2)
Demon's End (Tremble Island Book 3)